REVISIT THE PAST

Society of Swans
Book 3

Penny Fairbanks

Dragonblade Publishing, Inc. is an imprint of Kathryn Le Veque Novels, Inc.
P.O. Box 23
Moreno Valley, CA 92556
ceo@dragonbladepublishing.com

Produced in the United States of America

First Edition August 2024
Trade Paperback Edition

ARE YOU SIGNED UP FOR DRAGONBLADE'S BLOG?

You'll get the latest news and information on exclusive giveaways, exclusive excerpts, coming releases, sales, free books, cover reveals and more.

Check out our complete list of authors, too!

No spam, no junk. That's a promise!

Sign Up Here

www.dragonbladepublishing.com

Dearest Reader;

Thank you for your support of a small press. At Dragonblade Publishing, we strive to bring you the highest quality Historical Romance from some of the best authors in the business. Without your support, there is no 'us', so we sincerely hope you adore these stories and find some new favorite authors along the way.

Happy Reading!

CEO, Dragonblade Publishing

Additional Dragonblade books by Author Penny Fairbanks

Society of Swans Series
Awaken the Heart (Book 1)
Calm the Storm (Book 2)
Revisit the Past (Book 3)

CHAPTER ONE

April 1812

ISABEL'S REFLECTION SPARKLED in the tall mirror as she turned her round face from side to side. Sharp-green eyes examined every bejeweled and feathery detail as they caught the flickering candlelight. She took a step back, gloved hands brushing down the delicate, silver netting that overlaid her ivory gown, and nodded.

"Dearest, may I enter?" called a sweet, familiar voice from the other side of Isabel's bedroom door.

"You may," she replied. As the upper half of Aunt Matilda's face peered in, Isabel swirled around with arms spread out at her sides, making an ostentatious display of herself.

The lady's expectant smile transformed into a light laugh as she slipped into the room and closed the door behind her with a gentle click. The dowager countess's diamond-and-amethyst tiara glimmered amongst the midnight-black hair she shared with Isabel and Isabel's late mother.

"You shall be the star of Lord and Lady Lemmonbury's welcome ball, my beautiful niece."

She held out a hand and Isabel accepted, following along instinctively. Aunt Matilda turned her slowly as if in a dance.

"Are you prepared for another eventful Season?" Aunt Matilda prodded. She returned Isabel to her original position, nodding in satisfaction at the conclusion of her own examination.

Isabel's hand slipped out of her aunt's. Knowing the older woman would not mind her lack of decorum in private, Isabel shrugged and glanced down at the tips of her slippers poking out from beneath a hem embroidered in a silver feather pattern to match the feathers in her hair. The longest one drooped down and brushed against Isabel's forehead.

"Aside from the notable absences of Lydia and Felicity, it will be a Season like any other, I am sure," she answered with an unenthusiastic sigh as she quickly crossed to the chair in the corner and snatched up her reticule. Under her breath, with an equally unenthusiastic chuckle, Isabel added, "Unless another one of the girls receives a letter."

"Receives what?"

Every one of Isabel's muscles froze.

"Receives…offers," she hurried, fumbling with her reticule and pretending to take particular care that its contents remained exactly the same as when she had last checked.

"Whatever the reason," she continued in a nonchalant tone, "the tides of fate seem to have turned in my friends' favors this past year. Perhaps the matrimonial blessings will continue this Season. Now, we really should be off before little Maria attempts to stow away in the carriage and sneak into the ball."

Striding past Aunt Matilda toward the door, Isabel waved over her shoulder. She dared not look the other lady in the eye, lest she give away her and her friends' secret to that knowledgeable gaze, made wiser by life's experiences.

Though the Dowager Countess of Ainsworth was, in truth, Isabel's senior by only ten years—being the youngest sibling on that side with two brothers between herself and Isabel's mother— she had already lived a full life of courtships, love, marriage, and no small share of tragedy.

"Too right you are." Aunt Matilda chuckled. Isabel listened for the soft rustle of the lady's silk skirts as she crossed to join her niece at the door. Pausing, Aunt Matilda grasped Isabel's hand

and squeezed. "Whatever happens, I am sure it will be an exciting Season. They tend to find ways of making themselves so. Why else does the *ton* continue returning for this madness if not for the excitement that so often accompanies it?"

"Too right *you* are," Isabel agreed with a laugh, relieved to have avoided suspicion. She locked her arm with her aunt's and led them down the hall toward the stairs.

Isabel did not know what her chaperone and the only adult female relative in her life would think of some stranger contacting innocent neighborhood girls and sending them on wild hunts for romance, no matter how successful, nor did she wish to discover it. This was a mystery Isabel would not allow to be terminated prematurely...even if her active efforts at unmasking their anonymous matchmaker had understandably waned. She'd had more than enough to occupy her attention, what with the excitement and bustle of the past Season and the exhaustion of the ensuing period of recovery in the peaceful country, which had not been without its own drama.

She expected no such letter for herself. At least, she did not wish to be led down an imprudent path that would not ultimately align with her goal. Isabel had already delayed long enough and knew she must find a match for herself before Lady Swan might be tempted to intervene.

Perhaps this year, if one of her single friends did receive communication from Lady Swan, Isabel would renew her attempts to investigate. Between assisting Lydia and supporting Felicity last year, she had allowed herself to become too distracted from identifying Lady Swan. Besides, Isabel had yet to discover the correct method of interrogating someone to glean hints without exposing herself. Between her affable neighbors in Bainbridge and the tendency of rumors of any interest—including inquiries after a mysterious matchmaker—spreading like wildfire through the London gossip mill, it had proved too awkward thus far for much meaningful progress to be made.

In the foyer, they met with Papa, Lewis, and Maria. The

youngest Abbott glared over her shoulder at her governess, who lingered in the corner, ensuring the older woman respected Maria's right to see her family off for the evening and receive her deserved goodnight kisses. The animated little dear had argued quite effectively with Papa last Season, at just nine years of age, that she should be allowed that much if she was to be excluded.

"How pretty you look, sister!" cried Maria as she flew across the room. She threw her arms around Isabel's middle and smiled up at her, eyes shining.

A stirring glow of appreciation for the girl settled over Isabel. Squeezing back, she planted a swift kiss atop Maria's chestnut hair.

"Thank you, darling. If only I did not have to wait another eight years to see how pretty you will look on your way to a London ball."

"See, Papa?!" Detaching from Isabel and rounding on a heel in one swift motion, Maria jabbed a finger at their father. "Isabel thinks I should attend Lord and Lady Lemmonbury's ball! I shall only watch, I promise! And I will stay out of the way. Hardly anyone will notice me—"

"Heavens, see what you have done?" Lewis grumbled, his tall, slender figure perfectly framed by the front doors. "I would think you, of all people, would choose your words with more care. If you had, perhaps this one"—evidently amused, he jerked his head in Maria's direction—"would not have learned how to prod and argue so effectively."

A kind young man, though selfish in ways unsurprising of his age and sex, Isabel's brother was always the most eager to be on their way to any fun event. Conversely, he became endlessly preoccupied with every last insignificant detail of his fashionable dress and dark hair—never without a healthy heaping of pomade—when it came time for the dull ones.

"Well, now, I believe it is time we said our farewells," called Miss Oakley's measured voice. From the shadows, the governess appeared beside her charge. "We mustn't make your family late,

Miss Maria." She settled an appropriately firm hand on the girl's shoulder, a few fine lines appearing around the corners of dark-brown eyes as she smiled politely.

"Goodnight, my love," Papa said quickly as he rushed forward and took his youngest child in his arms, pulling her tightly against his portly frame. "I shall look into your room when we return, as always."

Stumbling along toward the doors after Aunt Matilda, one hand clutched in the dowager countess's, Isabel threw a promise over her shoulder of a thorough report on the ballroom's glittering decor and fashions. Inside the carriage, while Papa, Lewis, and Aunt Matilda chattered with enthusiasm about whom they expected to see in attendance, Isabel ruminated on her own expectations of the Season.

Dark, London streets lumbered past her window, obscured by a layer of glass and the deep shadows of nightfall. Aunt Matilda was correct. Isabel could feel it in her bones, though even her naturally pensive mind could not comprehend why.

The Season would be an exciting one, indeed…starting this very night, perhaps.

Only when the family emerged into the merry bustle of the Lemmonburys' ballroom and began lavishing their hosts in greetings and compliments did Isabel's churning thoughts finally return to the present.

"Finally! There you are!"

Isabel spun around at the sound of Clara's light, forever-carefree voice. A cluster of young ladies, resplendent in their finest gowns and brightest jewels, deftly wove around mingling guests and harried footmen toward the Abbott family from some unseen corner.

"Good evening, Lady Ainsworth, Messrs. Abbott," said Mercy, just loudly enough to be heard over the music and chatter. She and the other young ladies quickly dipped into curtsies.

When Isabel glanced up at Papa, she found him already nodding his permission.

"Go along, then. But do not wander too far from your aunt's watchful eye. Miss Reeve, Miss Gardiner, Miss Clara, wonderful to see you this evening."

The gentleman gave a rosy-cheeked smile and subtly shooed both his children away. He never minded managing the greetings while the young people set about the all-important quest of making a memorable night for themselves.

"I know, Papa." Isabel returned a fond chuckle of her own just as a familiar arm looped through each of hers. She was captured.

"May we borrow Miss Abbott?" asked Clara absentmindedly without waiting for a reply. She and Mercy turned Isabel around and began marching her toward the nearest sideboard.

"Enjoy yourselves!" Aunt Matilda called, quickly excusing herself from her brother-in-law to follow along after the girls at a comfortable distance and mingle along the way.

"You are beautiful, dear Isabel!" Clara squealed as they reached the farther and quieter end of the sideboard. The mountainous platters and towers of food afforded some privacy from the onlookers who sought entertainment outside of the dance floor. The younger Gardiner's pale-orange hair and the complementary emeralds woven through it blazed bright under the chandelier.

"I have missed you so since we last saw each other in Bainbridge," continued the youngest and most excitable member of their circle. "Tell me, what has been keeping you occupied since your family arrived in London?"

Laughing behind one hand, Isabel held up the other. "A moment of peace, I beg you. Or at least a moment to select some refreshments. I have not eaten a single morsel since breakfast, now that I think of it."

"The lemon tarts are lovely," offered Ellen quietly, her dark, doe-like stare darting to one of the trays piled high with pastries of all different flavors. "Come, sister, try one since you did not have an opportunity before Isabel's arrival."

Always happy to oblige the older girl, especially when sweets were involved, Clara wasted no time securing her own plate. She moved faster even than Isabel, plucking up every item her eager eyes landed upon. Despite their still-empty stomachs, the others could not help laughing at their friend's innocent antics.

"Can you believe it is the start of another Season?" asked Mercy after they had each enjoyed a few delicious bites. She shifted her weight from one foot to the other and back again, unusually restless, blonde curls bouncing. "It feels too strange with Felicity and Lydia still in the country…"

Instantly, Ellen abandoned her plate and came around to Mercy's side, the one usually occupied by Felicity.

"You poor dear, you must miss your twin terribly," Ellen cooed as she slipped an arm around the other lady's waist.

Mercy, normally poised with quiet confidence, lowered her head. "I have never experienced a Season without Felicity next to me at every single moment."

"Indeed, this shall be our first Season without our full ranks," Isabel mused.

She brushed away the crumbs that clung to her silken fingertips. Perhaps that was the strange feeling that had plagued her in the carriage on the way to the ball—that feeling of different days to come.

Of course this year would be different with two of their number, both wed last summer, remaining in Bainbridge. Calm, steadfast Lydia was busy preparing to deliver her first child any day now while bold, energetic Felicity still struggled to navigate the unpleasant symptoms of her newer condition.

Isabel's beloved friends were finally marrying and starting their families, turning to new chapters in their lives.

"Everything is changing so quickly…"

Mercy and Ellen nodded their agreement, both wearing small, bittersweet smiles.

"More change may be yet upon us! Who will receive Lady Swan's letter this Season?" Clara wondered aloud cheerfully as she closed her eyes and inhaled the spring aroma of the floral arrangement beside her.

Just as their youngest member's eyes and mouth opened again, most likely to expand upon her romantic notions, as she was wont to do, Mercy's and Ellen's gazes darted to something over Isabel's shoulder by the ballroom doors.

Ellen squeaked, her hands flying to her cheeks. "You mustn't look, Isabel!"

Isabel turned. Never had she regretted something so quickly. A strange feeling flooded her veins with boiling heat as her lips parted in unladylike shock.

Him.

The man once known to her as Mr. Caleb Smythe...her Caleb...now the Earl of Murfield.

A stranger.

His achingly familiar, deep-brown eyes pinned Isabel to her place. Or perhaps it was the waves of longing and disgust that crashed against each other within her heart that rendered her powerless to run.

The music and laughter and glamor faded away. He was far too close. How was he already so close?

The gentleman stopped at a respectable distance—the only respectable thing Isabel had seen him do. He lowered his head in a bow. His bright-red hair settled in subtle waves as he resumed his tall posture with a tight smile.

"Good evening, Miss Abbott."

Just like that, as if nothing had changed, as if years had not passed, as if her heart had not gone numb with the effort of suppressing her pain, Isabel's former suitor greeted her.

CHAPTER TWO

Miss Abbott. The name tasted strange on Caleb's tongue. He could not remember the last time he had used it. Even in his memories, she had always been Isabel...his Isabel. He needed to cleanse his palate, to chase away that terrible feeling that she would always be Miss Abbott to him now—at least until she took another man's name.

"May I have the next dance?"

His blurted words came as a shock to them both. Taking a step back, Miss Abbott's striking, green eyes widened in what Caleb could only describe as complete loathing. Her hands balled into fists at her sides. Why had his first instinct been to ask for a dance? Was he mad?

Of course he was. But somehow, Wrighthall had done an excellent job of convincing Caleb that the time had come to return to the world of the living, as any good friend must do after suffering through nearly four years of Caleb's grief-stricken running.

Yet even the glares he received from Miss Abbott's own companions failed to stop the rush of happiness that had enveloped Caleb's heart in a warmth he had not felt since that fateful day. It seemed time had not done much to lessen that sensation, no matter how far Caleb had gone to escape it—to escape all of it.

The lady's lips pursed. The shallow dimple in her chin almost disappeared from view.

"You may not," she announced without a hint of uncertainty in her voice.

Guilt followed quickly on the heels of Caleb's disappointment. He should not have been surprised.

How many times had he told Wrighthall that he would have been a fool to hope that Miss Abbott would accept so much as a smile from him? After what Caleb had done, he did not deserve even this much of her time.

"I understand. I pray you will forgive the impertinence," Caleb said in a rush, bowing quickly.

It was his turn to step back. This had indeed been a terrible mistake. He should never have attempted to return to Society, to Miss Abbott's life, as if he could possibly claim any place in either of them now. His weakness had forced him to give them up, and would send him all across the United Kingdom yet again.

"Isabel," whispered one of her loyal friends in a tone of caution.

Miss Mercy, Caleb guessed, given what he recalled of the identical Reeve twins' markedly different demeanors. From what he'd observed thus far, the other seemed not to have taken part in the night's festivities. The sixth young lady, Miss Dailey, was absent as well, or perhaps they were both occupied with full dance cards.

"If you refuse one gentleman, you must refuse all others," Miss Mercy continued, lowering her voice still further. "It would be a waste of the first ball of the Season…given your renewed interests."

"Of course, if you truly do not wish to dance with *him*, we would all understand," added Miss Clara Gardiner, grasping one of Miss Abbott's gloved hands in hers. Miss Gardiner merely peered at the commotion from behind her younger sister.

All the while, Miss Abbott's hard stare remained fixed on Caleb's burning face. Standing completely still in her breathtaking beauty, she did not look inclined to alter her decision. Caleb lowered his head once again, spurred more by shame than by politeness.

"I should be going," he mumbled.

"Good. I would rather not dance at all than dance with you."

Caleb flinched as her words came down like blows from a hammer. Painful as they were, he knew he deserved them.

"My apologies," he repeated, turning in defeat.

Caleb had only managed a few steps, forcing his broad shoulders to squeeze between two happy couples prancing toward the dance floor, when he halted in his tracks. A gloved hand had snatched his wrist. A hand he would have recognized anywhere merely by its weight.

Heart in his throat, traitorous hope flickering, Caleb faced her. Miss Abbott dropped his hand as if he'd burned her. Her eyes fell from Caleb's to the floor.

"I was so dreadfully sorry to hear the news of your brother…"

"Thank you, that is very kind," Caleb replied quickly.

His jaw tightened as the line reverberated in his mind. It had been in frequent use since his unexpected reemergence in London. The *ton* had not had an opportunity to offer their condolences at the time of his older brother's death, nearing on four years past.

Almost no one had seen or heard from the new Earl of Murfield since. He could hardly bear to be seen or heard now. Not when his heart still felt so tied to his loss.

A moment of awkward silence stretched between them, drowned out by the simple pleasures of a dazzling evening. Guests filtered past them, eager to dance and converse and feast while they remained still, frozen in time.

Caleb's stomach twisted. Would it ever be any other way between them now? Would they ever enjoy such a night together again, even just as something resembling friends?

"I heard," Miss Abbott began under her breath before pausing. Her gaze darted about at the sideboard, the overflowing flowers, the delicate, swirling pattern of golden moulding along the walls—everywhere but him.

"Yes?" Caleb leaned forward instinctively.

"I heard through the gossip mill that you have been enjoying extensive travels throughout the country, and even to parts of the Continent and the Americas. Many were under the impression that you had no desire to return to life amongst the *ton*."

She paused again. This time, her eyes found his. Caleb almost recoiled at all that remained unsaid in them.

"It seems I am in need of a change in scenery for the time being. Indeed, I had quite forgotten the merits of such lively Society." Caleb glanced out at the ballroom, fit to burst with the *ton*'s finest.

After another, shorter pause, Miss Abbott gave a curt nod, black curls catching the blazing candlelight. "I am at least pleased to see that you are alive and well."

"Miss Abbott, I truly cannot begin to say how sorry—"

"Please." She held up a hand and Caleb gladly fell silent. He looked down at his polished shoes. His words had sounded inane and futile even as he'd spoken them.

"I do appreciate your apology, but I have managed just fine thus far without it. I wish you the best, my lord."

Caleb winced at the sting in her voice. There was a goodbye if he'd ever heard one. Miss Abbott spun around and stormed back to her friends, who encircled her in their protective arms and ushered her to a distant corner.

As he watched her go, that flicker of hope that had teased the back of his mind since he'd decided to resume his life turned to ash.

"That was not a success, I take it?"

Frowning, Caleb refused to look at the gentleman who had appeared at his side. "What could have possibly given such an impression? I should not have allowed you to influence me into this."

Wrighthall's hand settled on Caleb's shoulder and began steering him back toward the doors. "I am sorry, my friend, truly.

I hoped there might be a chance."

As footmen closed the ballroom doors behind the two gentlemen, Caleb rounded on the baron and threw his hands up. "Why should there have been?"

His friend shook his head, his perfectly sculpted brown hair remaining quite firm, and mirrored Caleb's frown. They fell into step together down the dark hallway.

"Well, as you recall, the Season after your abrupt disappearance, I heard that Miss Abbott had made clear her intentions to seek a match of material comfort rather than love."

"I do recall, yes. Is that not still the case?" Caleb inquired, grimacing into the flickering shadows cast by the sconces lining the walls.

Wrighthall sighed and let one foot land heavily on the first step down to the foyer. "That is just the thing. Though I have not said as much…"

He paused and threw a glance at Caleb from the corner of his eye. Caleb's grimace deepened, this time at himself.

It had been four years since he'd been forced to leave Miss Abbott behind—since he'd made the greatest mistake of his life.

He'd handled it all like a complete blockhead, though perhaps some of that might have been excused by the surrounding circumstances if Caleb had had the gentlemanly courage to be more forthcoming much sooner. Because he seemed incapable of releasing the pain of losing both Miss Abbott and his brother, Caleb had inadvertently forced Wrighthall to continue treading carefully around either subject.

"Speak freely, please. If this reunion—if it can be called as much—is any indication, I hardly imagine whatever information you impart will increase my disappointment by any great degree," he said with a sigh, listlessly waving one hand.

His friend paused in the foyer and looked about. "Miss Abbott, being highly accomplished, pretty, and agreeable, and from a well-connected and respectably rich family, has not been without her share of interest from the *ton*'s bachelors."

Feigning a sudden fascination in a speck of dust soiling his otherwise-pristine lapel, Caleb turned away and made thorough work of dislodging it. He had been wrong. Wrighthall's words, and the flashes of images they conjured in his mind's eye, did pierce his heart.

"Is that so?" He managed to force through gritted teeth, pretending not to hear yet another long-suffering sigh from his closest and oldest friend, at least since Daniel…

"Yes," Wrighthall continued patiently. "But, as far as I am aware, she has never accepted any of them as proper suitors—no matter their qualifications."

Caleb's heart, so used to limping along, battered and exhausted, went still. "Is that so?"

"Your carriage, my lord," announced a footman who seemed to have appeared from thin air mere feet from Caleb's face.

"Thank you. Please give my apologies to Lord and Lady Lemmonbury that I have been called away so soon."

To Caleb's great relief, Wrighthall did not leave him in suspense. The moment the carriage door closed behind them, throwing them into the darkness of its velvet interior, the baron resumed.

"For whatever reason, Miss Abbott ultimately seems to find some excuse to dismiss every man who signals his interest. She has done this for the past three Seasons. You pride yourself in your intellect, yes, Murfield? Does that not strike you as odd behavior? Perhaps it is time for something to be done about it."

The carriage lurched forward. Caleb allowed himself to sway with the rhythm of the horses' movements, his gaze drifting out the window, the world beyond shrouded in mystery. He could not bring himself to hope again, not so soon after being soundly put in his rightful place.

"Perhaps they were all beasts. Or vapid. She would not marry a vapid man for all the wealth in the world," he mused under his breath.

Wrighthall chuckled and leaned back into the plush seat. "I

would say the latter is far more likely. But think of it. Surely, not each and every one has been quite *that* tedious."

"And what of the beasts?"

"You know I keep watch over her, per your request. No beasts have set upon her. Besides, I have every reason to believe that Miss Abbott's good sense would make quick work of removing her from such company."

"Then…what is the point at which you have been attempting to arrive?"

"Am I not permitted to hope for a dear friend's much-needed happiness?" the baron teased in a grumble.

Caleb huffed a short laugh without looking at Wrighthall. "Not if it is false hope. Given the evidence I have collected with my own eyes and ears from the lady herself—which clearly supersedes your speculation, I am afraid to say—any hope in that direction can be nothing but a falsehood."

"What if it is not false, after all? Why else would she refuse every gentleman when she might have been very comfortably settled by now?"

Wrighthall's rebuttal hung in the air for the remainder of the ride back to Caleb's townhouse. While he turned those questions and the events of the ball over in his mind, Caleb silently appreciated his friend's choice to tilt his head back against the upholstery, close his eyes, and doze.

The earl leaned his forehead against the cool glass. The shifting shapes reflected in it somehow seemed to configure themselves into Miss Abbott's features, still lovely despite the hatred etched in her soft lines.

No, there was only one conclusion that remained. If Wrighthall had seen her expression more closely, his hopes would no doubt be as dashed as Caleb's.

CHAPTER THREE

A NEAT ARRAY of sliced ham and egg stared back at Isabel as she poked it listlessly with her fork. She had coerced herself into taking at least one bite of everything on her plate and one sip of tea, hoping that her sleepless night of tossing and turning would have resulted in a healthy appetite.

Such was not the case this morning. Resigning herself to her stomach's blatant refusal to feel hunger, Isabel fell back into the plush embrace of her pile of pillows and settled her fork onto her pearl-inlaid breakfast tray. Byrd, her motherly lady's maid, would silently frown when she came to collect her mistress's uneaten meal, especially after Isabel had claimed a terrible headache resulting from too much frolicking at the welcome ball.

"What does Byrd know?" Isabel grumbled to herself as she indulged in her rarely seen childlike side and burrowed deeper beneath her blankets, crossing her arms over the lace ruffles of her nightgown.

No, the lady's maid—nor anyone else, for that matter—could not know that Isabel had spent the entire night reliving those few strange moments with the man she had once loved. That was one topic of conversation she could not bear first thing in the morning. Knowing Papa and Lewis, who had heard of Lord Murfield's brief presence from other guests, they would be curious as to her feelings on the matter.

Isabel scrunched her nose and shook her head, as if that could banish the memory of how handsome he had looked with his bold, red hair that never stayed quite flat and his deep eyes that never failed to captivate her…even after all this time.

It was infuriating, really, that he should look so precisely the same as she remembered from their days of courtship. As if he had not shattered her heart and disappeared from her world, only to reappear in London without so much as a hint to Isabel.

The childish stubbornness slowly dissipated from her expression as she forced herself to remember her hard-won lesson. What else could she expect from a man who would do such a disgraceful thing as run away with an innocent girl's love without looking back?

A different type of stubbornness seized Isabel. This one originated in that deep, dark corner of her traitorous heart that she had never quite been able to seal away. It shuddered now, pushing against Isabel's harsh opinions of the earl's character.

Isabel gritted her teeth. Had she not learned her lesson, after all? Had she not experienced any growth as a being of reason during these years after learning to live with her dejection? How could a few minutes in Lord Murfield's presence undo the walls Isabel had so carefully built around her scarred heart?

A soft knock on the door jolted Isabel out of her frustrated thoughts. "Mail for you, miss," called Byrd through the door.

"Enter," Isabel replied, settling the tray along the edge of her bed.

"Miss Abbott." The maid sighed as she closed the bedroom door, her attentive, blue eyes immediately landing upon the young lady's uneaten food.

"I am sure I shall be famished by the time luncheon arrives," Isabel promised with a sheepish smile as she accepted the letters from Byrd.

After a few more insistences that she wanted for nothing else, Isabel leaned back into her pillows once more and eyed the first letter. A smile tugged at the corner of her lips. Felicity's slanted, hasty handwriting announced itself loudly across the first letter, recognizable anywhere.

"...and with all this newfound energy since that terrible churning in my stomach seems to have ceased, I had begun to really regret not joining you all in London. Until Lydia told me more of what is to come. The comforts of Bainbridge seem far better suited to—well, I suppose you shall read about that the next time Lydia writes..."

Intrigue hummed inside Isabel's chest as she skimmed the remainder of Felicity's letter and snatched the next one. It was indeed from Lydia, her handwriting far neater, an exact copy of her governess's lessons.

"Our healthy, happy little Mary has arrived, and with her comes a joy and love like I never thought possible. She is sheer perfection..."

"Thank the heavens!" Isabel cheered quietly to herself, reading on.

She pressed the brief letter to her chest. The happy news from both her friends, but most especially of Lydia's baby girl and assurances of the new mother's growing strength, had done wonders to revive Isabel's spirit.

Until she brought the next letter to her eyes.

Her leaping heart sputtered to a stop. She would also know this handwriting anywhere thanks to the hours she had spent rereading her friends' mysterious letters in her mind, searching for clues...or perhaps simply enjoying the puzzle of it all.

And now one had arrived for Isabel. With a huff, she pursed her lips and turned over the folded sheet to reveal the telltale swan, stamped in purple. Isabel ran a fingertip over the raised wax and frowned.

This letter would contain nothing useful for her unless Lady Swan intended to point her in the direction of a tolerable, comfortably wealthy gentleman who sought a spouse for practical reasons, just as Isabel planned on doing.

It should have been her plan from the beginning. She would have saved herself much suffering. Instead, Isabel had had the misfortune of meeting the most incredible, most infuriating man she'd ever known during her very first Season.

Since the disappearance of the then-Mr. Caleb Smythe, Isabel had made it her goal to set aside any considerations of love in the marriage business. It was, after all, a business affair in many crucial ways.

Isabel had even found a few contenders who had all possessed the means of keeping Isabel and her future children secure and respectable in Society. Yet they had all fallen short for one reason or another. It was hardly Isabel's fault if they did not appear to be compatible even on a platonic level or, worse, if they ended up deciding that they did want to be in love with someone.

Or perhaps it was because…

Isabel shook her head again, harder this time, her nightcap struggling to stay pinned in place. Surely, given Lady Swan's two successes that Isabel had witnessed last year, she could trust the anonymous matchmaker to know what she needed. Granted, despite the strangely intimate knowledge Lady Swan seemed to possess of their lives and personalities, neither Lydia nor Felicity had been particularly convinced at the start that the mysterious letter writer had been leading them in the correct direction.

No, surely, within this note contained hints of the perfect, practically-minded man. Isabel steeled herself and broke the seal.

"Dearest Miss Abbott, welcome back to London and what I pray will be a fruitful Season for you. If you are reading this, I am pleased to announce that you are already well on your way. Thank you for trusting me.

"For the ability to trust—both in ourselves and in those around us— is one of the most essential components of a truly happy life. This fact is all the more essential when one's trust has been broken."

Isabel paused, squeezed her eyes shut, and let her hand and the letter drop to her lap like a brick. The tentative interest that had been twisting her stomach froze over in an instant. She need not read any further to know what Lady Swan implied. Still, her innate drive to understand every piece of information the world had to offer spurred her to resume with knitted brow and clenched teeth.

"If you are still reading, I thank you again."

Feeling entirely too old as a woman of two-and-twenty to be even momentarily consumed by irrational fears, Isabel stopped once more and pulled her blanket up to her chin. She glanced about her tastefully appointed bedroom. Now she could appreciate for herself that feeling that her friends had described upon the arrival of their letters—the feeling of being watched, heard, understood, but without knowing how.

"Once compromised, it may seem impossible for trust to ever be renewed. Pain takes its place and taints lovely memories. And while there are, of course, instances where such faith is best not renewed once betrayed, there are others where a different perspective may do wonders to bridge the gap of confusion and hurt.

"Above all, I pray you will remain open to a little-known truth: Past pains may lead to a lifetime of joy when two broken hearts heal as one.

"Allow yourself to set the practical matters aside. You deserve the happiness and companionship your heart desires, and the gentleman who loves you wants nothing more than to make your every dream come true.

"Your most loyal servant, Lady Swan."

Isabel's hand curled into a fist, crushing the letter in it. Hot, angry, childish tears stung the corners of her eyes as her chest heaved up and down. How dare this stranger try to convince her that the very man who had broken her heart should be the one to heal it? The very notion was absurd!

Whatever else Lady Swan might have known, however she had managed to know it, there could be no way for her to have any idea of the pain Isabel had suffered, which had been made all the worse because she had not been the only one hurting.

Several months after Lord Murfield had disappeared, failing to return after a promised few days of business outside of London, the shocking news of the late earl's unexpected passing had begun trickling through Society in hushed whispers laced with sordid fascination and a polite amount of pity.

When Papa had somberly relayed the tragedy to Isabel after hearing of it from someone at Brooks's, her tattered heart had broken anew. The previous Lord Murfield, the present's older brother, had been far too young for his fate. Isabel had known that her former suitor must have been grieving terribly.

Without much conviction, Isabel tossed the crumpled ball of paper away and sighed as it tumbled down to her powder-blue blankets and snagged upon the fine fabric.

Indeed, if the new earl had reached out to her then, perhaps Isabel would have still been tender enough to accept an apology and administer comfort to someone who had once been so very dear to her, so principle in both her easy, idyllic thoughts and her careful plans of the future. Perhaps it could still be so... Would there truly be much harm in it?

A surge of restless energy took hold of Isabel. She flung the thick blanket back and swung her legs over the side of the bed in one deft movement. She'd already paced two or three laps up and down the room by the time the bedcover had finished settling into careless, lumpy peaks.

"No!" she said in a sharp whisper as she kicked out the frilly hem of her nightdress, in a rush to get nowhere in particular. "I was young and it was all too much to bear back then. I am older and, hopefully, a little wiser now."

No matter what her silly heart or anonymous writers had to say. Isabel finished that thought silently to herself. There were things that need not be said aloud, not even in the privacy of her own quarters.

"Besides," she continued aloud, eager to leave those thoughts behind, "should not Lady Swan, with all her mysterious powers, know that Lord Murfield clearly has no desire to remain in Society properly? Of course, why should he? Gallivanting about the country is far more entertaining and stimulating than an endless repetition of Seasons in London. No doubt that friend of his, that Lord Wrighthall, bullied him into finally showing his face."

After several more intervals of sullen silence and acrimonious mutters against both Lord Murfield and Lady Swan, Isabel's initial agitation subsided long enough for her wits to return with a course of action. Thankfully, her mind had continued to work to her benefit under the surface while she had allowed herself a few moments of unbridled emotion.

Reaching across her unkempt bed and seizing the letter, Isabel made quick work of smoothing it out enough for Lady Swan's admittedly handsome writing to be legible. She settled in at the carved, oak writing desk in the corner of her room and produced a tidy stack of quarto sheets from the right-hand drawer.

Stretching her neck from side to side in preparation for a long period of sitting, Isabel dabbed her pen into glossy, black ink.

"Dearest Lydia, all my congratulations and blessings to you and Sebastian and your darling Mary! I cannot tell you how thrilled I am for you and how anxious I am to see you all happy and well with my very own eyes…"

Isabel's quill flew across the blank page, populating it in an endless, effortless flow. Her skills at crossing her letters would be put to the test if she hoped to convey her well wishes in addition to the entirety of Lady Swan's message, not to mention her own opinions, of which there were *many*. The need for more pages quickly became evident as she crossed every line up, down, and diagonal.

Still, Isabel knew her friends in both London and Bainbridge would be more than happy to offer up a few extra pence to learn that their hopes of Lady Swan's continued involvement in their circle had not been in vain.

CHAPTER FOUR

"S HE IS HERE!" Clara cried as the butler showed Isabel into the Gardiner family's drawing room. Without a second thought, she tossed her embroidery hoop aside, leaving it to clatter against the thin rug and dull floor beneath, and flew to Isabel's side.

"My poor sister was beginning to think you actually *had* taken ill. She has become so impatient," added Ellen, following behind the youngest Gardiner at a calmer pace. "Come now, dearest, let us allow our friend to seat herself." She offered Isabel a sweet, apologetic smile as she grasped Clara's narrow shoulders and began steering her back toward the sofa and chairs arranged in the center of the drawing room.

Observant Mercy patted the empty space beside her on the sofa with long, lace-covered fingers. Isabel obeyed, sinking into the upholstery with some measure of relief. It was not as though she had not kept herself in as much suspense as her companions these past few days. In fact, her reticule sat heavily on her lap, each letter within like a rectangle of brick rather than finely woven cotton.

"Forgive me, all of you," Isabel started as Clara pressed in close on her other side and Ellen tucked herself into the protection of the late Mr. Gardiner's favorite wingback chair.

"It was not my intention to torment you with waiting, but I did not think it sensible to tear apart our busy schedules numerous times when we could simply have one long discussion now that all the relevant information has arrived. Besides…"

Clara, affectionately clinging to Isabel's arm, tilted her head to one side, pale-orange curls swaying. "Besides?"

Isabel tore her eyes away from her friend's expectant gaze, full of romantic dreams. "Besides, I wished to reduce my chances of crossing paths with Lord Murfield at the larger dinners and dances."

Mercy reached over to grasp the hand not already claimed by Clara and cleared her throat. "On the topic of Lord Murfield, perhaps we should refresh our memories with a reading of Lady Swan's letter, which I presume you have brought with you?"

Nodding, Isabel rummaged in her silk reticule for the first letter, the one that had begun it all—the one that always began it all.

"Would you do us the honor of reading it aloud?" she asked, brandishing the neatly folded sheet before Clara's doll-like face. Her friend eagerly snatched it and began reading the words Isabel had long since memorized and often shuddered to recall.

"I am afraid your assertion must be correct, Isabel," said Mercy when Clara had finished, one finger tapping thoughtfully against her knee. "Who else can Lady Swan mean but the earl? Thus far, the first and obvious guess has proven to be the right one."

"And Lydia and Felicity, what did they make of it?" Ellen asked, leaning forward slightly, brown ringlets perfectly framing her delicate features.

With a sigh, Isabel produced the remaining letters. "Naturally, I brought their responses with me as well."

"How perfect!" Clara cheered, bouncing in her seat a few times. "It is almost as if our dear friends are here with us, after all."

"Heavens, I had half a mind to request that Nicholas return us to Bainbridge so we might meet precious Mary. The first baby among us!" Ellen said with a meditative smile as she wrapped her arms around herself.

"You know our brother would never have granted your request," Clara retorted with a pout. "He would think it a waste of his beloved money and time, both of which are clearly better spent here in London."

"*Clara!*" Isabel hissed in surprise, her head turning sharply toward the younger girl before looking to the eldest.

It was no secret that Mr. Nicholas Gardiner, their older brother, saw his status as head of their household as simply that—status, and access to the luxuries it afforded, nothing more. His responsibilities entered into his mind only when the poor girls forced them to.

Thanks to Ellen's seemingly endless ability to see the good in others and Clara's natural desire to impart her own carefree cheer on all she met, the sisters preferred to express their disapproval in brief, veiled comments. In fact, Isabel could not remember the last time she had heard either of them use such bold complaints against anyone.

Ellen sank deeper into their father's chair. "Do not mind her," she whispered, cheeks coloring. "Nicholas and Clara have argued again, and it has confined Mama to bed with nerves. He says we will not have our pin money this month because, well, he did not explain precisely, but…"

Isabel and Mercy exchanged a knowing glance and pursed their lips to keep from saying anything unladylike about a friend's relative, even if said friend would no doubt heartily agree.

The other Bainbridge ladies had heard enough talk of Mr. Gardiner's spending habits through their own families without the help of hints revealed by the sisters since their father's passing. The Bainbridge mamas had also never seemed particularly keen to marry their daughters to him despite being a gentleman from the neighborhood, not if that gentleman was so careless with his purse strings.

"Shall we hear what our friends at home have to say about all this?" asked Mercy in her measured, tactful tone. The sunlight spilling in from the large windows cast her golden hair in an angelic glow. In the absence of their leader, Mercy had naturally assumed Lydia's role as their sensible guide and reminder of decorum.

With a sulking scowl, Clara sat back against the sofa cushions, which were beginning to show the need for some maintenance. Nothing urgent yet, though certainly something the Gardiners' more sharp-eyed guests would begin noticing while Mr. Gardiner brushed it aside as inconsequential compared to the winnings he could earn on the next boxing match.

Ellen gave what appeared to be a small smile of relief that the subject had been proposed to change, and that her younger sister did not seem intent on resurrecting it at present. "Will you not read again, dear Clara?"

Curiosity no doubt compelling her, as it always did, Clara reached one hand out and accepted the two letters Isabel placed in it, her glowering expression already reduced to a mere scrunched nose.

"I shall read Lydia's first. I am terribly eager to learn more of her little one and what it was all like."

"Temper your expectations now," Isabel interjected. "She does not share much on that subject. I suspect it was too much to write in a letter, even with multiple pages crossed every which way. But she does describe her Mary in wonderful detail. You will be pleased," she added quickly upon seeing the disappointed drop of Clara's eyes.

Excitement renewed, Clara took a deep inhale and began reading.

"'...and she grows a little stronger and more alert by the day, with dark hair, dark as her papa's, beginning to show. She is so small, yet I cannot comprehend how my body sustained her for so many months. How she could begin as a dream and become this real, breathing creature in my arms. How we can love this little stranger with hearts that have expanded to sizes we did not know possible. And to see Sebastian as the wonderful father I always knew he would be! It is the most sublime *feeling, and I pray all of you will come to know it in your turn.'"*

"Motherhood has turned our solemn Lydia into a poet," Isabel said with a fond chuckle as Clara finished the first half of the letter.

Clara pressed the quarto sheets to her chest and sighed wistfully. "May it make poets of us all! She sounds *so* thrilled that I cannot help being thrilled as well."

"I am now even more eager to return to Bainbridge and meet the little dear! But what does Lydia say of...?" Ellen paused, her round eyes darting nervously to Isabel.

Isabel softened and smiled at quiet, kindhearted Ellen. "You may say his name. It is not a grave sin. Only a minor one."

The other girl, so truly sincere, demure, and unguarded, chuckled and relaxed, her shoulders rounding ever so slightly. "What does Lydia say of the Lord Murfield theory?"

"Ah, yes." Clara cleared her throat and continued. "*'I know you will not wish to read this, Isabel, but I believe your suspicions are correct. I cannot think who else Lady Swan might mean. But I hope my example, and Felicity's, will bring you some measure of peace. I am too content with my life now to continue wondering how the woman manages to be right. I only know that she is, and I believe with the entirety of my being that she will not steer you wrongly. Might you find a sliver of possibility in your heart that Lady Swan's reasoning is sound and trustworthy?'"*

"Well, might you?" prodded Mercy as she leaned back slightly for a better view of her friend's face.

Instinctively, Isabel turned away and feigned a sudden interest in the table, particularly in the green, floral pattern that wrapped around the rim of her teacup. Heat simmered under the surface of her cheeks, no doubt turning her face a color that was entirely too honest, though not for the reason she had expected.

She was not, exactly, embarrassed to talk about *him*—Lord Murfield, she reminded herself, just as she had reminded Ellen. Not like during her first Season, when she had revealed every detail of her courtship with Mr. Smythe to her dearest friends with bashful smiles and hopeful whispers of the future that had been just there on the horizon, secure with a comfortable allowance and property long ago promised to him by his brother, only to watch it sink behind that line forever.

Everything had been so fresh and exhilarating then, for Isabel and for the other Bainbridge girls. Though she ultimately had not been the first—or even the second—among their number to marry, Isabel had been the first to experience any sort of courtship or romance.

Isabel ignored the gentle jab in her side from Clara's elbow. This was different. Isabel was different.

Despite the admittedly absurd, almost-fictional situation she had found herself in, Isabel could hardly deny the fact that she was no longer that innocent, impressionable girl of four years past. She had been so sure that she would never again allow her logical mind to be compromised by false promises made to her fallible heart. And yet…

She also could not deny that feeling deep in her chest, warm and familiar, a feeling she had long since thought lost to her.

It had shaken off its cold slumber as soon as she'd seen the regret in Lord Murfield's eyes at the ball, even if her resentment had prevented her from recognizing it in the shock of the moment.

It had softened the walls around her heart, the ones she had erected *because* of the man Lady Swan—and all Isabel's friends, apparently—wished to see her marry.

The evidence was clear. Whether Isabel liked it or not, the matchmaker's abilities had been proven twice over now, in two very different situations. The others believed in the evidence. Only Isabel now struggled to do the same because the evidence posited a possibility she did not wish to accept. And with good reason, or so she had thought.

Worst of all, she *missed* Lord Murfield. No, not Lord Murfield. She missed her Caleb.

"What did my sister write?" Mercy finally asked after another long moment of silence and another unsuccessful nudge from Clara's sharp elbow.

Happy to have something to occupy her once more, Clara took up the last letter and quickly read through the older twin's report of her ever-changing condition.

"'*Naturally, I agree with whatever Lydia thinks. No doubt she wrote it out far better than I ever could. We are all grateful I have been spared the task, I am sure. But truly, Isabel, you know that I, of all people, wanted absolutely nothing to do with Lady Swan and her schemes. And look at me now! Happily married to the kindest man with a little one on the way. I cannot tell you how she does it, but Lady Swan possesses a magic all her own. She knows what you need better than you do.*'"

When Clara read the last line, Isabel's fingers curled around the folds of her creamy-orange walking dress. She may not have been raised as rigidly as Lydia, or been born as blindly hardheaded as Felicity, but Isabel still did not take kindly to accepting that she might have been mistaken. Especially on such a crucial matter.

"There, that settles it!" Clara announced as she folded up Felicity's letter and returned it to Isabel along with the others. "We all agree that Lord Murfield *is* the intended gentleman and that there must be at least *some* merit to our writer's suggestion. Truly, Isabel, do not you think it at least worth it to discover why he did not return for you or write all this time?"

"*You* all may agree," Isabel interjected before Clara could lose herself in a cloud of fanciful dreams, "but I do not see why I *must* do anything simply because Lady Swan—and a bunch of silly girls—ordain it."

"It is not silly to be optimistic for our friends' futures!" Clara sat up straight, crossed her arms, and tossed her head at Isabel's teasing.

With that, the conversation devolved into more jests and lighthearted speculations as to the unfolding of Isabel's adventure, to which she listened with more amusement and interest than she cared to admit. Nor would she admit to any of them, not yet, that the sliver of possibility did exist in her heart.

Perhaps it had never truly been erased.

✣

AS SOON AS Isabel stepped foot into the foyer of her family's townhouse, she paused, one glove hanging limply in her hand. Something felt different.

"Swinton?"

The butler, just beginning to gray from his years of service, sprang forth in anticipation of his young mistress's question. "Two visitors await you in the drawing room, Miss Abbott, as well as your aunt."

"And who are our unexpected visitors?"

Swinton's professionally neutral expression wavered. Isabel narrowed her eyes.

"Lady Ainsworth requests that you come up straight away upon your return."

"I am afraid I do not much care for the sound of that," Isabel mumbled under her breath. Turning to Swinton, she added, "Thank you. That will be all for now."

The butler offered a bow and left Isabel in the privacy of the foyer. Curiosity and apprehension battling for dominance in her thoughts, she stood tall, straightened her shoulders, and marched up the stairs.

"Ah, here she is now!" called Aunt Matilda's sweet, feathery voice.

The two men had not yet turned to the new arrival when Isabel's every muscle froze. She would never be unable to recognize Lord Murfield's fiery hair and broad shoulders, it seemed. They had certainly haunted her memory often enough to leave a lasting impression.

The earl and Baron Wrighthall, his closest friend, gave some sort of greeting. Isabel could not hear it for the sudden rushing of blood in her ears. She forced herself into a curtsey and, without allowing her gaze to linger on the gentleman on the right, rushed to the dowager countess.

"Might I have a word, Aunt?"

The older woman fixed the younger with a firm look that Isabel could not quite decipher. Her green eyes—deeper and certainly wiser than Isabel's—darted to their guests.

"Surely, it can wait a while longer, my dear Isabel," Aunt Matilda countered with a lighthearted chuckle. "Do become reacquainted with Lord Murfield, darling. He has come all this way to call on you. Isn't that lovely?

"Besides," she added, raising her voice for the benefit of the others, "I just remembered hearing that Lord Wrighthall is an admirer of fine accessories. I thought he might like to admire your father's handsome pocket watch display! Am I not mistaken, my lord?"

"Indeed you are not, my lady. I very much enjoy a painstakingly curated collection," answered the baron with a smile that struck Isabel as a touch too eager to be entirely natural.

Her jaw tightened as Lord Wrighthall offered his arm to Aunt Matilda and allowed her to direct him toward the long, glass case that stretched across the opposite wall. The lady looked over her shoulder at Isabel with an apologetic smile.

Isabel bristled internally at the necessary politeness to which she typically did not mind adhering—except for when she must extend politeness to a man who had cruelly hurt her beyond anything she had thought possible. She also bristled against the familiar stare she felt upon her back that had once sent shivers of warm delight through her entire body.

It wanted something of her that she could not possibly be ready to give. Everyone wanted this of her—Lady Swan, her friends, perhaps even Aunt Matilda.

But none of them understood. Not really. How could she doom herself to a lifetime of wretchedness by walking with eyes wide open into a repetition of history?

This ambush had done nothing short of snuff out the meager stirrings of hope she had secretly begun to entertain at the Gardiners' home, her friends' confidence lifting her up. Or perhaps it was easier to think of reuniting with Lord Murfield when he was not so…close. So real. Such a reminder of the dreams she had not realized she'd desperately wanted until they had disappeared like smoke.

"Miss Abbott, I hope you have been well?"

Isabel swallowed around the lump of conflicting emotions in her throat. There was nothing for it now. She could not run forever.

Somehow, she had not been expecting the awkward, regretful, and unfortunately endearing expression on the gentleman's unfairly handsome face as she turned. From several steps away, Lord Murfield watched her with wide eyes, his angular brows upturned at the corners.

Isabel did her best to ignore the stuttering of her heart. This cautious version of the earl was so different from the friendly and sharply intelligent young man she'd known, always prepared to debate his views or discuss recent readings with any like-minded individual. Yet there was something about this Lord Murfield that forced Isabel's hardened heart to twist back into shapes she thought it had forgotten.

Yes, Isabel stood before her former suitor as a different person. But life had changed him, too.

"Come now, my lord. We need not revert all the way back to such basic conversation," she finally said. "We do know each other, after all. Even if it has been some time."

Lord Murfield's tense, perfectly full lips gave way to a small smile and a light chuckle. He dropped his head in relief, thick hair shimmering in the sunlight that poured in from the window.

This time, Isabel did not ignore the fluttering spasms in her chest. Life had changed him, indeed. She found herself longing to know all that had come to pass—to understand how his presence could feel so familiar, as if they had never parted, yet so much heavier.

Could this truly be the same man with whom she had fallen in love *and* come to loathe all in the span of a few months?

"So, tell me…" she continued as she took a step forward, surprising both herself and Lord Murfield. Their eyes found each other at the exact same moment. "Why are you here?"

Her question contained no bite or accusation. It had taken less than half a moment for Isabel to feel the truth of her own earlier statement. No matter how long it had been, no matter how much she had tried to convince herself, their history could not be so easily forgotten.

Lord Murfield lowered his head again and cleared his throat. "I know I have no right to make such a request of you, and if you choose to decline, you shall have my full understanding, but…"

When he did not continue, Isabel felt her foot lifting of its own accord once more. She took one step, then another, until she came close enough to peer at his hidden face, head tilted to one side. Deep-brown eyes slowly lifted to meet hers.

"Continue," Isabel said quietly, gently.

"I ardently hope, Miss Abbott, that we might resume…our friendship. You see, I have never stopped admiring you from afar, all these years. Throughout all my journeys, you remain the most fascinating and wonderful person I know, if I may be so bold."

"I suppose you may," Isabel whispered as the breath left her body in a surprised exhale.

She could feel her eyes widening and her cheeks reddening, and she was powerless to stop herself. He had always known precisely what to say—often without realizing it—to make Isabel's knees weak.

"Perhaps it might also help to know that I do not expect I shall be returning to London again for quite some time, I should think, after the Season. Thus, you shall not have to endure me for long," he continued with a sheepish smile.

Just like that, the generous feelings that had begun taking

root were singed by disappointment. They retreated into the darkness, where they clearly should have remained. Isabel hummed thoughtfully in the hopes of securing enough time to dispel her instinct to decline his offer and excuse herself, just as she had done at the welcome ball.

It was not as difficult to manage this time thanks to that cursed spot of softness that had been worked into her heart via the urgings of Lady Swan and Isabel's own beloved companions. Indeed, in taking a moment to allow her mind to turn over the positives and negatives, Isabel found that the definitive time limit of Lord Murfield's presence in her life could prove beneficial.

If she could not bear to be in the same rooms as him and converse civilly before the attentive eyes of their friends and the rest of the *ton*, at least she would have the comfort of knowing that the earl would soon disappear from her life once more.

The nervous rustle of his coat called Isabel out of the labyrinth of her thoughts, a place in which she often lost herself. Lord Murfield had once loved losing himself there alongside her.

The gentleman shifted his weight from one foot to the other, tugging at the cuffs of his sleeves. "Forgive me," he mumbled without looking at Isabel. "I knew it was a mistake to ask."

"I suppose I can accept a temporary friendship," Isabel blurted out just as Lord Wrighthall appeared in the corner of her eye, rushing toward them with long strides.

"Murfield, we have lost all track of time," he announced, brandishing his own pocket watch. "I am afraid we must be making our way to White's, or we shall keep our friends waiting."

The earl's Adam's apple bobbed, his lips parting for just a moment before pressing into a tight line. As the gentlemen offered their thanks and farewells to the ladies, Isabel could not help another twinge of disappointment. After all, had she not been waiting for him, too?

With the drawing room door closed, Isabel shook the thought away, curls swinging. It was far, far too dangerous to entertain.

"Will you tell me what you and Lord Murfield discussed?"

Isabel turned to the sound of Aunt Matilda's voice with what she hoped was a nonchalant shrug.

"We are friends again, it seems, at least until he resumes his escapades when the Season is finished. If he does not quit the Season early. That would not be entirely unheard of from him."

The other woman smiled softly and wrapped an elegant arm around Isabel's shoulders. The emerald green of her skirts and the light orange of Isabel's clashed against one another as the women made their way to the pair of chairs under the window.

"That was very mature of you," said Aunt Matilda in a reassuring tone.

Isabel only nodded. In a flash, the pride in her aunt's eyes transformed into a curious glint.

"This is as close as Lord Murfield will ever be allowed to come near my heart again," she announced quickly and firmly, perhaps as much for her own benefit as Aunt Matilda's. "He made it abundantly clear. Soon we shall be strangers once more."

Though her shapely brows inched up, evidently intrigued, the dowager countess always seemed to know when to leave certain lines with her niece uncrossed. "Fond strangers, I hope," was Aunt Matilda's only reply on the subject.

"I suggest that you do not allow your hope to grow unchecked," Isabel grumbled, this time more to herself than to her aunt.

As she watched the leisurely walkers and carriages passing on the street below, Isabel vowed to repeat her own words to herself as often as she must until they became a permanent impression upon her heart. This meeting had ultimately served to reinforce her original position.

It did not matter what Lady Swan thought. Isabel and the Earl of Murfield were not meant to be. If they had been, he would not have been walking away from Isabel now, leaving her to wonder when, if, she would see him again.

CHAPTER FIVE

S IGHS OF INTEREST rippled through the small group of old and new acquaintances that surrounded Caleb as a stream of words spilled forth from his mouth. The dinner guests nodded along, absorbing every unique detail of the many beautiful estates—preferably uninhabited or with absent owners—he had encountered during his years of exploration.

Yet again, Wrighthall had been correct. This was the price Caleb must pay for his years away from Society. Stories.

If he did not wish to admit his true reasons for disappearing and racing around the United Kingdom, that was. He doubted the *ton* would care to hear much about the mist of tears through which he'd viewed the marvels of Stonehenge in Wiltshire, mourning the absence of his dear brother, who had accompanied Caleb on a previous visit and unexpectedly fallen in love with the mysterious ruins.

"What a fascinating eye you possess, Lord Murfield!" cried one gray-haired gentleman, raising his teacup. "The way you describe your travels with such vibrancy makes me regret overlooking these magnificent, ancient places here in our very own country during my youthful travels around the Continent. I suppose I could not hope to manage such a tour, even a domestic one, at my time of life."

Caleb chuckled and shook his head. "Not at all, Mr. Stanhope. With a sensible route, ample time afforded for travel and enjoyment of each location, and carefully made arrangements that are suitable to your particular needs, there is no reason you should not make an adventure for yourself yet, I promise you."

"Particularly if you were to arrange it, my lord," added a woman Caleb recalled meeting during a previous Season.

The now-Lady Ramsbury pressed a silken hand to one angular cheek, blue eyes sparking. "How knowledgeable you are of the most singular places, with all your peculiar little facts, and how to best arrive there!" she continued, her enthusiasm growing as an idea appeared to strike her.

"Have you considered applying your experience in aid of others who wish to become more acquainted with our United Kingdom? If I could but introduce you to my younger brother, I am sure he would be so much safer and have a much more enjoyable time with such a guide!"

"Goodness, you are far too generous in your estimation of my talents," Caleb said with an appreciative smile and bow of his head. He swallowed, silently praying that the young viscountess's suggestion had not been so serious that a refusal couched in humility would be ignored, and that no one else would champion the idea.

Of all the many small surprises Caleb had encountered since his return to Society proper—from long-lost friends suddenly married with children to old, favorite establishments transformed in the blink of an eye—he had not expected the *ton* to be so curious about his expeditions, about him.

He sensed, to his displeasure, that his long absence and intentional avoidance of company in favor of supposed deep self-reflection and intellectual expansion had created an air of mystery about him that attracted the *ton*'s curiosity. At least with their focus transfixed by a stimulating subject, Caleb need not worry as much about their interest turning to more morose matters like Daniel.

"Mr. Abbott and Miss Abbott!"

The butler's robust announcement drove every other

thought and concern out of Caleb's mind. He took a breath before turning toward the drawing room door, lest he look too quickly, too eagerly. Besides, he did not feel eager at present, exactly.

There stood Miss Abbott in a lovely, powder-blue gown threaded with silver, diamonds twinkling in her black hair. She held herself tall as her clever eyes swept about the drawing room. Against his wishes, a memory overlaid itself upon the present scene.

It was the first time Caleb had seen her truly enter a room, at a dinner much like this one, drawing all the light to her. They'd met only two days prior at a picnic in Hyde Park, where they had quickly discovered a mutual love for the philosophical poetry of William Wordsworth.

Caleb watched Miss Abbott and her father greet the evening's hosts and a few others nearest the door from across the room. Only when she looked directly at him did Caleb realize that he had been staring far too intently.

Old habits were difficult to break, so they said. Difficult, though hopefully not impossible. The Season had only just begun a week ago and already, Caleb wondered how he would survive it. He turned back to the others to find that, during his distraction by the new arrival, they had dispersed to other corners of the drawing room.

"Enjoying your evening, Lord Murfield?"

As always, Miss Abbott's lovely voice threatened to envelop Caleb in a happiness that no longer belonged to him. These feelings rushed back far too naturally. It had been foolish to think that he could return to life in London while avoiding her. He had barely managed it this long.

"And here I thought we were friends," Miss Abbott continued, her tone flat except for the lilt at the very end. She was only teasing. Then why did her words leave Caleb's skin stinging with shame?

He forced his feet to turn him around to face Miss Abbott's

beautiful visage.

"We are, Miss Abbott," Caleb answered. "If that is still agreeable to you."

"If it were not, I would not be standing here."

She smiled. Caleb's heart melted. This was a mistake, indeed.

As long as he remained in town, he would never be free of the memories they shared. Seeing her unexpectedly at this dinner necessitated a new plan. Caleb must quit London early and resume his tour of England's hidden gems…or venture farther afield, perhaps to the Americas.

"For that, I am grateful," said Caleb, painfully aware of how deeply he meant it and how badly he longed to escape all at once.

"Might we sit?" Miss Abbott inquired. She glanced over to a pair of chairs by the fireplace. "I am afraid I danced entirely too much at Mr. and Mrs. Rutledge's ball last night. My poor feet nearly refused to carry me to the breakfast room this morning."

Caleb readily agreed as they took their seats, trying not to think about the men with whom Miss Abbott had danced and if any of them possessed the correct attributes to finally entice her into another courtship.

"Now, where was I? Ah, yes. You still have not answered my first question. Are you enjoying your evening?"

For some reason, Caleb did not answer. Instead, he observed Miss Abbott observing him. Her gaze remained fixed on him, hard, almost distant. Despite her valiant attempt at fulfilling Caleb's request for friendship, she could not quite hide her own struggle to find normalcy in their situation. Not from him.

Yet again, he had been pensive and silent too long. The lady's pleasant smile grew tighter and she lowered her head. Perfect, inky curls swished against her prominent rouged cheekbones. Caleb's heart thudded against his ribs as a wild, familiar urge nearly compelled him to reach across the small table between them and tuck a ringlet behind her ear, to feel the softness of her skin against his fingers just as he'd once done.

Somehow, it felt both like a lifetime ago and just yesterday.

"Forgive me. Perhaps we had better not—"

"Tell me, what have you been reading?"

Miss Abbott's head lifted sharply. Her eyes were no longer distant. In fact, they enchanted Caleb entirely.

"You did remind me that we need not bother with the pleasantries. As friends."

"It might be easier to tell you what I have *not* been reading," she answered with a light chuckle. "Luckily for you, I always carry this with me."

Her notebook. Caleb already knew before she produced the small volume from her silver-beaded reticule.

"My notebook. I write down any interesting passages I encounter, if they are short enough, or else leave a reference and page number so I might copy the full quote in my larger book at home. It makes for quite a handy tool to keep track of my reading."

Miss Abbott proudly brandished one of her most prized possessions before him. He made note of the plain, indigo leather cover and furrowed his brow. The one he remembered had been forest green. It had contained the glimpses of Isabel—revealed in bits and pieces in those pages and in the pages of every work she recommended—with which Caleb had fallen in love.

Vitality and openness returned to her eyes—not fully, yet enough to provide him with a taste of that brilliance and insightfulness he adored and had missed so, so terribly. No one in this country, nor even the world, he reckoned, could dive headfirst into discourse like Miss Abbott.

"Recently, I have found myself drawn to the epistolary style and have just begun reading *Evelina* again. That, along with my other studies, keeps me busy during whatever down time remains to me after these long days of engagements."

Caleb nodded, unable to suppress a fond smile as he listened to Miss Abbott's enthusiastic reviews of her recent literary interests and their effectiveness in her pursuit to broaden her mind.

"I do recall your admiration for Fanny Burney's keen eye and wit. There is something rather charming and intimate about epistolary novels, is there not? After all, we are always telling the stories of our lives in letters."

Miss Abbott stilled. Her features softened as she stared at Caleb. A tingle of uncertainty rippled through his stomach, his hands curling into loose fists atop his knees. Perhaps they were not yet comfortable enough to reference their past so freely.

"Thank goodness we live in the age of letters, and may it reign long," she answered quietly after a long moment. "Now, enough of my simple comings and goings. I would be most grateful to hear more of your exciting tales—if you are not fatigued from recounting them to your other friends, that is."

Caleb pressed his lips together to keep from frowning. Odd. Miss Abbott, a skillful conversationalist and highly adept at expressing her many fascinating, complex ideas, did not often rely upon such rapid changes in conversation topic.

Time seemed to have done nothing to erase his ability to sense the subtle changes in the lady's mood. From the corner of his eye, Caleb noted the sudden twisting of her hands in her lap, the twitching tendon at the base of her neck, the flicking of her gaze from his face to anywhere else in the drawing room.

The cause of these nerves, however, remained a mystery to him. One he was not likely to be successful in solving with this new foundation between them in such a tenuous state.

"Luckily for you," Caleb replied as he leaned across the arm of his chair, borrowing Miss Abbott's earlier phrase with a playfully arched brow, "I saved the most exciting tales for your benefit entirely."

The tension in her genteel figure eased and she smiled in an expression that looked to be a mixture of relief and disbelief. Miss Abbott waved a dismissive hand through the air.

"Of course you did not! Why should you have? I saw them flocked around you when we arrived, and I have heard talk amongst the *ton* of your engrossing stories."

Caleb could not help himself or the levity bubbling up in his chest. He laughed for the first time in what felt like months—years, perhaps. He certainly had not had occasion to laugh like this. Not since the last time he had shared a carefree day with his Isabel.

"What you and I deem engrossing and what most of Society as such finds the same do not often intersect, I am afraid," he finally managed to huff out as his laughter subsided to a chuckle.

This unexpectedly light feeling remained as Miss Abbott's smile widened to match Caleb's. If any of the other dinner guests mingling nearby noticed their slightly unrefined expressions, clearly neither Caleb nor Miss Abbott cared.

As always, it felt as if they existed in a world all their own.

"And I am afraid I am inclined to agree with you," she said, the trace of a laugh in her voice.

"Most of what they wish to hear primarily pertains to any luxuries I experienced," Caleb confessed with a shrug of one shoulder.

For a flash of a second, Miss Abbott scrunched her face, the charming dimple in her chin deepening.

"Horrid." She sighed, shaking her head. "Of course, you and I know that the real fascination is to be found in the history not only of the land, but of those who have tended it. I pray you have much to tell of both?"

Caleb could not tell if his companion was aware of how she leaned closer in her chair, looking up at him with round, earnest eyes, or how dizzy it made him to have her so near and so absorbed in their conversation. A mere week ago, Caleb had been certain that that very same lady would rather swim across the Channel than share a ballroom with him ever again.

"I must begin with the Salisbury Plain in Wiltshire. What magnificent archeology! We are truly blessed that such testaments to our ancestors remain accessible to us these many millennia later all throughout England, but I assure you, you cannot begin to imagine the likes of Stonehenge."

"Or what it must feel like to stand in the very same place as someone from ages past, living an entirely different life, and imagine what the world was like in their time," she added, thoughtfully tilting her head to one side.

Caleb smiled. "Precisely."

Now, as he took his turn and shared the true marvels of his many journeys, sparing no seemingly tedious detail that he knew his present audience would appreciate, Caleb could not help feeling as though nothing much had changed between them, after all.

How many times had they talked just like this, in various drawing rooms, ballrooms, and parks, stealing every opportunity to share recent discoveries and opinions and, all the while, tender bits and pieces of their innermost natures?

"Ah, it is time to move into the dining room!" called their hostess all too soon. Caleb had not yet finished describing the particularly diverse insect life fostered by the area's grasslands.

"Miss Abbott?" he asked as he rose from his chair, extending his hand to the seated lady.

Without looking up, she held up one hand, while she ruffled inside her reticule with the other. For half a breath, Caleb feared that she'd found herself in need of smelling salts or a handkerchief after all his talk of creeping and crawling things, as most other ladies would have. Instead, her other hand produced a pencil. She leafed through the pages of her notebook and scribbled something in the next clear space, under what looked to be a quote copied from *Evelina*.

"There, so we shall remember where we left our conversation," she announced with a pleased nod, tucking her items away once more. Bright-green eyes snapped up to meet Caleb's common brown ones. "I *must* hear more about Salisbury Plain's insect life—about all of it."

When Miss Abbott accepted his hand, Caleb felt as though she had never let go.

A moment later, to his great disappointment, she was compelled to release him as their hostess, Lady Huntingford, paired them with guests more befitting each of their ranks for the entrance into the dining room. Caleb's disappointment only increased when Miss Abbott's escort led her all the way around the long, mahogany table. He settled into his own seat, situated diagonally from hers. At least it afforded him a pleasant view of her lovely countenance and superior grace, though there was nothing to be done about the floral centerpiece that occasionally obscured her.

"Lord Murfield, I am so pleased to be seated beside you. I have heard much talk of your time visiting the great sites of England and am eager to hear more directly from the source!" said the guest seated to Caleb's left.

When he turned to face his dinner companion, he nearly jumped. The friendly lady, a recently pronounced spinster from the prominent Montbray family, leaned forward to catch his attention. She blinked her pale-blue eyes at him expectantly.

Caleb gave an appreciative nod. "I would be delighted to divulge anything you wish to know—at least of the places I have been. There is still much to see of this country and the world beyond."

He could not help himself. Caleb's gaze drifted across the table to Miss Abbott once more. Miss Montbray's first question, something about the dullness of traveling primarily alone and staying in empty houses, drifted in one ear and out the other.

As long as he shared a room with Miss Abbott, she would never be far from his thoughts. And if she was the primary object of his thoughts, how could he hope to pay mind to anything or anyone else? He could have given his entire life to the study of her every breath.

"My lord?"

Caleb started and forced his attention back to the woman beside him.

"Many apologies, Miss Montbray. I must have been distracted by that strangely orange dish in the middle of the table," he lied with a sheepish smile. "As to your inquiry, you may be surprised at the ways one can occupy oneself without companions and parties."

The remainder of the meal passed relatively uneventfully. Miss Montbray and Mrs. Johnson, on Caleb's right, proved quite effective at distracting him from staring across the room at Miss Abbott all evening and wondering what she discussed with the gentlemen seated beside her—with no small amount of effort on Caleb's own part. He had forgotten how difficult it had been to focus during those early days of all-consuming infatuation. Every ounce of his energy went toward maintaining the necessary connection with both his dinner partners.

As much as Caleb longed to return to the solitude of travel, he did not wish to offend anyone along the way, especially since time seemed to have softened the *ton*'s indignation at his very unceremonious departure from their world. Instead of being met with disgruntled politeness, he had been welcomed with open arms…by all but one.

When the time came for the ladies to return to the drawing room, Caleb took advantage of the commotion to observe her every movement. The way she walked with measured strides and had a smile and kind word to offer every guest who came near, the way her fair skin and dark hair reflected the light from the chandelier—it was all perfection. He had walked uncountable miles and still never encountered a more beautiful woman.

"I do hope you are not thinking of courting her, Lord Murfield."

Caleb spun around on his heel to face Mr. Dunn, one of his newer acquaintances, heart thumping in his throat. "Who?"

The other man, the eldest son and heir to a great fortune, made lesser by its lack of accompanying title, lifted his glass of port toward the adjoining door as it closed behind the last lady.

"Miss Abbott, of course. You are acquainted with her, are you not? That is what I have heard, and in any case, you do seem on quite friendly terms, if I may say so," answered Mr. Dunn as he smoothed his blond hair with a palm.

Tendrils of cold dread crept out from the center of Caleb's chest and slowly seeped to the rest of his body. He swallowed, yet his heart refused to dislodge itself and return to its rightful place.

"I am acquainted with Miss Abbott, yes. We…knew each other before I began my travels."

Mr. Dunn tilted his head back ever so slightly to eye Caleb properly. "But you are not courting her?"

"Indeed not. I have no intention of planting roots that may threaten to bind me to any one location." Caleb shook his head a touch too forcefully. A few gentlemen chatting nearby glanced at him curiously from around their drinks.

Luckily, Mr. Dunn seemed too lost in thought to notice, a bejeweled finger tapping his chin. "Then perhaps you might know if she has been entertaining any other suitors?"

Caleb shook his head again, this time with hard-won composure. "Not that I am aware of, no."

Mr. Dunn nodded. "What do you make of her character?" he continued in a practical, unsentimental tone. "I have heard that she is extremely accomplished, even for a lady of good breeding. And there can be no denying that she is quite pretty, do you not think?"

The question twisted Caleb's stomach around itself. He snatched a glass from the tray of a passing footman and took a generous sip, praying it would douse the uncomfortable heat building under the surface of his skin.

"Certainly, I suppose anyone would think so."

"I am sure they must," agreed Mr. Dunn with growing enthusiasm. "It would be exceedingly advantageous to marry a woman who brings distinction to me as her husband not merely through her accomplishments, but through her beauty as well." He added in a sly whisper, "Is it wrong of me to enjoy imagining my friends' shock if I were to secure a handsome wife?"

Caleb bit down hard on the inside of his cheek, his hands tightening into fists at his sides. He forced a tight smile onto his face.

"Of course not. A man should take pride in his wife. Just as every woman should take pride in her husband. As to Miss Abbott's character—"

"Ah, yes, yes." Mr. Dunn laughed, waving a hand through the air. "Is she truly as proficient in the ladylike arts as they say?"

It took every bit of resolve Caleb could muster to summon a satisfactory answer that would deservedly extol Miss Abbott's virtues while keeping hidden his unwarranted jealousy. Of course that was the source of the heat ravaging him from head to toe and the horrible ache in his stomach that would double him over the moment he was alone.

Yet again, he could not help it, no matter how desperately he longed to remember that he had no right to harbor such a feeling. His foolish heart would not allow him to release it.

"Whatever you have heard, I can assure you, does no justice to the truth."

"Is that so?" Mr. Dunn's mouth pulled down in an impressed sort of frown, the glint in his eyes growing sharper. "Pray tell me more."

Ignoring everything inside him that screamed that this was not right, Caleb did as he was bid.

"Miss Abbott is the superior example of every quality any lady may hope to possess. Whether it be extensive reading, the study of languages and history and art, the practice of every fashionable skill from embroidery to painting to pianoforte, she excels at them all, not only because of her natural intelligence and talent, but also because of her dedication to constantly improving herself."

"Very good, very good," Mr. Dunn mumbled under his breath, nodding along, eyes narrowed.

"But, perhaps even more importantly," Caleb said, compelling himself to continue, "Miss Abbott is also the superior example of every noble virtue any lady, and indeed any man, should hope to do honor by emulation. Her kindness, patience, integrity, and charity are second to none."

"Excellent," said Mr. Dunn quietly.

Caleb glanced at the other man. Mr. Dunn's look of eager consideration faded as he gripped his chin.

"If I may offer any further assurances, I would be more than happy to do so," Caleb quickly offered.

Of course, he did not desire to do anything to bolster Mr. Dunn's interest, yet he also could not allow there to be any question about Miss Abbott's suitability for marriage. Caleb had already ruined enough of her future.

"Since you seem so familiar with her temperament, you do not think she would become…disagreeable?" Mr. Dunn sighed and shrugged. "You know how these young ladies can be. Sometimes, if they are *too* bright… Well, it can lead to an obstinate nature, now can't it? That is one thing I should very much like to avoid in a wife—"

"You need not entertain any fears on that score, sir," Caleb said in a rush, dragging each word up his raw throat. A bead of sweat that had collected at the nape of his neck dripped down into his starched collar. "I have every reason to believe that Miss Abbott understands perfectly well what is expected of her."

The tension in Mr. Dunn's thin face eased. So much so, in fact, that he clapped a hand upon Caleb's shoulder.

"Thank you, indeed, my lord. Miss Abbott does sound like precisely the sort of girl I—or my mama, rather—have been searching for."

Caleb bit the inside of his other cheek this time. "And what have *you* been searching for, if I may ask?"

Mr. Dunn exhaled sharply and gave Caleb a commiserating smile that he did not share. "You know how mothers can be, too, no doubt. Now that I am nearing my thirtieth year, she has grown more insistent that I marry soon. Never mind the fact that I am doing no different than any other gentleman! What fellow is ever in a rush to shackle himself?

"Still, I have recently come to realize that once I appease dear

Mama, she will no longer have reason to meddle in my affairs. Taking all you have kindly shared—and the other information— into consideration, I believe she shall suit the office just fine, indeed. Above all, I desired to know that she would leave me to my freedoms without quarreling. It sounds as though she will, based on your recommendation."

"'Other information'?" Caleb repeated, his brows knitting low over his nose as he attempted to ignore the rest.

"Ah, you have been absent for quite some time, my lord." Mr. Dunn chuckled. "It is quite common knowledge these days that Miss Abbott prefers much the same as I do. As long as she leaves me to my peace and eventually provides an heir, I shall leave her to her pursuits. Does that not sound like the ideal arrangement?"

Caleb gave a smile that felt more like a grimace, his nails digging into the meat of his palms. "I am sure it shall bring you much joy."

But not Isabel…

Of that, he was confident. She may have convinced the rest of the *ton*—even herself—that she would settle. Caleb could not be so deceived. Not with all he knew of her, all he had seen of her wonderful heart.

Miss Abbott would never be truly happy with a match in which her partner had no intention of sharing her interests or hearing her thoughts. Her material requirements would be sated, but not her intellectual and emotional needs.

With a *thud*, the adjoining door opened. The time had come for the men to rejoin the ladies in the drawing room. And not a moment too soon for Caleb.

"Lord Murfield, do recommend me to Miss Abbott, if you would not mind," called Mr. Dunn as Caleb's powerful legs carried him swiftly toward the door.

The other gentlemen spilled in slowly behind him and dispersed. One of them approached Miss Abbott and another young lady, conversing happily by the curtained window. Thankfully, the man led away the latter for a private word of their own.

Caleb's body moved of its own accord once more, taking advantage of the opportunity. He crossed the room and paused before Miss Abbott.

"I sense that you did not enjoy your port as thoroughly as you would have liked," she said. Her eyes widened as they took in what must have been quite a harried expression.

"I would have much rather continued our discussion of Salisbury Plain's insects." Caleb sighed wearily and rubbed at his jaw with a hand.

Miss Abbott stood a little straighter, curiosity returning in full force to her gaze. "We may continue it now, if you would like. But first…"

Pausing, she glanced over Caleb's shoulder. He did the same and immediately chided himself. Seated in the middle of the room with an optimal view of the window, Mr. Dunn watched them intently. Caleb had known it would be a mistake to entertain the man's queries and feed his hopes for as long as he had.

"I believe Mr. Dunn is attempting to catch your notice for some reason," Miss Abbott whispered, artfully angling her face away.

Caleb huffed a wry chuckle. "Not *my* notice, but yours, Miss Abbott."

"Mine?" She wrinkled her nose, fingers pinching her skirts.

"He requested that I recommend him to you."

"And do you?"

For a long, quiet moment they stared at each other. Miss Abbott's brow twitched up at the corners, a silent encouragement.

"He seems to match your criteria, and he assured me that you would be allowed to live your life as you see fit while he does the same."

The words tasted wrong in Caleb's mouth. Instead, he should have cried out with all the air in his lungs that there could be no world in which Mr. Dunn would bring Miss Abbott the happiness she truly deserved, even if she thought she did not want or need it.

Then again, Caleb had failed at that, too.

Miss Abbott's eyes narrowed. "Why are you telling me this?"

Caleb could only etch a tight smile onto his face. "Because this is what good friends are meant to do—support each other in reaching their dreams and goals."

Though her gaze softened as she glanced over her shoulder once more, she did not appear particularly enthusiastic when she turned back to face Caleb again. Her curved lips, a pretty, pink hue, came together in an endearing pout.

"You are very kind to say so, but Mr. Dunn... I do not think it likely." She gave a gentle shake of her head, so imperceptible that surely the gentleman in question would think nothing of it, if he noticed it at all from this distance.

Relief should have flooded Caleb. Yet he could not bring himself to be quite pleased about the shadow of disappointment cloaking her soft features.

"May I ask why?"

The strange question slipped from his lips before he could stop himself. Miss Abbott looked down at the few inches of plush rug between their feet. The tops of her full cheekbones reddened.

"Because...he is simply not right."

All of a sudden, her eyes flew up to meet his. Caleb nearly stumbled back at the intensity flashing in them. The burst of wild hope it ignited deep in his chest disappeared just as quickly.

"Pardon me. I just thought of something I must ask one of my acquaintances over there," she mumbled, dropping her eyes again and hurrying away.

Mr. Dunn half-rose to his feet, triumph alight in his eyes.

"Ah, Miss Abb—"

She kept her gaze down and rushed past his seat, pretending not to hear, toward a group of young ladies. The man's head whipped around to Caleb, his mouth still open with his ignored greeting.

His only reply was a subtle shrug and an apologetic frown. Even from here, he could see the exhale Mr. Dunn heaved. Luckily, he did not seem inclined to pursue the matter further and abandoned his chair in search of other prospects.

Caleb remained in his spot for several long moments, content to watch Miss Abbott converse with the girls who had cheerily welcomed her into their circle while he feigned admiration for the craftsmanship of a delicate porcelain vase.

No, he was not content, exactly. Perhaps he should have been, given her adamant statement against her potential suitor. Yet as he lingered here with hands clasped behind his back, so close to the object of his heart's desire yet so removed from her life, Caleb did not feel at ease.

Mr. Dunn was not right. *And neither was Caleb.*

He knew her well enough to hear the unspoken in her words. Caleb's fingers squeezed tighter around each other as he attempted to rationalize with himself. There must have been some way to control his feelings if he hoped to maintain any sanity during the Season, whatever remained of it.

After all, even if Miss Abbott had rejected Mr. Dunn tonight—and had turned away who-knew-how-many other hopefuls during the past few years—eventually, someone would win her hand, whether by her choice or by necessity. He sent up a silent prayer that he would be long gone from this place before he must be forced to witness it.

After all he had borne in his life already, Caleb knew he did not have the strength to bear that.

CHAPTER SIX

B IRDS SANG, SUNLIGHT shone in full force, and a sweet, spring breeze tickled the back of Isabel's neck as she swayed in time with the barouche. The distant chatter and light laughter swelled into a cheerful cacophony the closer they came to Gunter's busy street. Isabel looked out over the open side of Aunt Matilda's carriage, allowing the neat rows of townhouses and fashionably dressed passersby to distract her from her own thoughts.

As they turned onto the street, a most welcome sight met her eyes. Sitting taller, Isabel lifted a hand to chest height and gave a small wave. The driver skillfully parked their barouche along the side of the teeming street behind the carriage containing Mercy, Ellen, and Clara.

"Do enjoy yourself, my dear, and be mindful not to drop any ice on your gown," said Aunt Matilda, patting Isabel's knee.

"You are not joining us?" Isabel asked over her shoulder as a footman helped her down, the dowager countess following. Aunt Matilda glanced at the other carriage of young ladies and gave them her usual tranquil smile.

"Later, perhaps. For now, I wish to stretch my legs a while with a walk. Never fear, for I am never far," she added in a teasing whisper.

A familiar intuitive glow in her eyes, she reached over to swiftly pinch the younger woman's cheek. With that, Aunt Matilda took her parasol from her footman and began her leisurely pace down the pavement.

"Isabel, come join us!" Clara's airy voice drifted to Isabel on the wind, followed by a gently mumbled reminder of decorum from Mercy.

Another footman assisted Isabel into the Reeves' exceedingly handsome burgundy landau. She perched upon the empty place beside Clara.

"Now, who should like to begin?" asked Isabel after they had dispatched their orders to the staff.

The other three merely stared at her for a moment until Mercy said, "I am sure we are all most interested in your endeavors of the last few days."

Ellen's nod of agreement was modest compared to her sister's, whose bright-eyed enthusiasm threatened to send her ribbon-trimmed bonnet flying into the street to be trampled by all manner of carriages, carts, and horses.

"Has he called on you yet? Surely, he must have! It has already been a week since he last visited! I say, what could possibly be keeping him from you?"

The words flew out of Clara's mouth in one enthusiastic breath. Isabel could not help the sudden, overwhelming desire to shrink away from her friends' curiosity. Knots twisted in her stomach. She knew what they would say when she revealed their unexpected encounter at last night's dinner party.

Though Isabel had never suffered much in social situations, being the focus of such attention felt foreign, almost invasive. Especially when Isabel herself could hardly make any sense of her ever-changing emotions. Every time she came near enough to grasp hold of one and investigate it, it mutated, turning her own well-worn arguments—whether for or against Lord Murfield—into strangers. More often than not, Isabel's exploratory endeavors into her own mind left her with increasingly convoluted doubts in both directions.

Clara gasped and threw a hand over her mouth. "He *has* called on you, hasn't he?"

Even the generally composed Mercy and reserved Ellen leaned forward, their gazes fixed on Isabel's face. She pressed herself deeper into the cushioned corner of the landau.

"Not quite," she answered. "He happened to be in attendance at Lord and Lady Huntingford's dinner last night."

"So he could speak with you?" Mercy prodded.

Isabel quickly shook her head without making direct eye contact with the other girls.

"I should think not. He seemed as surprised to see me as I was to see him. In fact, whatever he said last time he called on me, I am sure I would not have heard from him again had we not crossed paths last night."

"How can you be so certain?" Ellen added quietly, hands twisting in her lap. "Perhaps he is simply...shy."

That thought had crossed Isabel's mind in her more generous moments. She waved a hand at Ellen's suggestion and her own misgivings.

"Then why would he request a friendship in the first place?"

"Please, will you not tell us what happened?" Clara pleaded, her warm, brown eyes round and bottom lip pushed out.

"I will not," Isabel announced with a smug smile.

Just as Clara opened her mouth to beg again, Isabel tilted her head to the side. The others looked and, for a blissful moment, fell happily silent. The footman had returned with their ices. They each savored the first bites of their treats with satisfied sighs.

"Do you really mean you will not tell us how the dinner went?" Ellen asked as she dabbed at the corners of her mouth with a kerchief.

Isabel paused, her next spoonful of delicious, chilly maple halfway to her mouth. "I will, but only after I hear from each of you first."

The young ladies agreed, Clara with another pout, and took their turns alternating between enjoying their ices and listing off the engagements that had kept them occupied since their last meeting.

"As I am sure you all might guess, Lady Eldmar has sent me out to as many events as she can find space for in my diary," Mercy began as she stuck her spoon into a slowly melting mound of elderflower ice.

Isabel and the others nodded their sympathies. Though she would never dare admit as much, Isabel could not help noticing the faint shadows that had taken up residence under her friend's eyes recently, made invisible at present only thanks to the shade from Mercy's bonnet.

"Two nights in a row of balls, one with the Bakers and the other at Almack's. Every day, there has been either a luncheon or dinner party, and in between, I was subjected to carriage rides and trips to the Egyptian Hall and Somerset House and Astley's," she finished with a weary sigh.

The poor twins had suffered a lifetime of their mother's neglect until last Season, when it had come to the viscountess's attention that some among the *ton* had found it odd that her two youngest children were still unmarried. Since then, in an effort to insulate her own reputation, Lady Eldmar had made it her most crucial mission to send Felicity and Mercy down the aisle. With the former unexpectedly settled, the full weight of the viscountess's efforts had fallen upon Mercy's narrow shoulders.

"Perhaps it is time you feigned ill for a few days," suggested Clara, wearing an encouraging smile that did not quite possess her usual optimism. "Surely, even her ladyship will allow you some rest then."

Mercy chuckled and reached across to grasp the younger girl's free hand. "I am afraid I may soon have no choice but to take your suggestion. And what of you and Ellen?"

Eyes widening, Ellen quickly slipped another spoonful of chocolate ice into her mouth and fixed her sister with a stare. Unsurprised, Isabel and Mercy turned to Clara for the report from the Gardiner household. Clara frowned down into her dish and absentmindedly chipped away at her favorite pistachio treat.

"Mama does her best to bring us out as much as possible, but you know Nicholas. Since last we met, he has only allowed us the carriage once, for a dinner at Mrs. Frampton's. I am beginning to fear that unless one of you is always disposed to convey us about London, we shall never again see anything but the walls of our home."

"You know we will answer your call as often as we are able," Isabel promised quietly around the tightness in her throat.

She also could not help noticing the sisters' increasingly worrisome complaints of their older brother's behavior and wondering with no small amount of anxiety at what would become of the dear girls as his habits became unsupportable.

"But…"

All attention turned toward that sweet, demure voice. Ellen continued to stare at Clara expectantly. The younger lady's head whipped up and to the side, eyes sweeping across the bright-blue sky as if suddenly noticing its lack of clouds. Before Isabel could probe any further, brows furrowed, Ellen continued.

"Clara forgot to mention that the younger Mr. Dailey was in attendance at Mrs. Frampton's dinner. It appears he himself has just returned from his most recent journey to Wales and has stopped in London for a week or two before making his way to Bainbridge."

"He said he was so thrilled by Lydia's news," Clara continued through pursed lips, "that he ended his trip early and left his friends in Cardiff to come meet his niece—but he decided to recuperate from the travel in London and allow the little family more time to themselves before Mary's buffoon of an uncle arrives. That was his precise wording, not mine," she added quickly, glancing over her shoulder at her friends.

Isabel and Mercy shared a surreptitious look of their own but, as usual, refrained from commenting when the topic of Lydia's younger brother was touched upon in Clara's presence.

"There, now it is your turn, Isabel," Clara announced, nodding sharply.

Isabel could only sigh and accept her fate. She cradled her dish in both hands and rested them in her lap. "The dinner last night was…not terrible. In fact, it was pleasant. Quite."

"That sounds promising," said Mercy in a cautious tone.

"Hardly." Isabel scoffed. "It was pleasant in a purely amicable manner. After dinner, Lord Murfield even attempted to earn my favor for another man, at the request of said gentleman, that Mr. Dunn."

"Could that not be because you have given him no signals that might encourage hope?" asked Clara, eyes ablaze once more. "Surely, he must believe there is no chance of your ever being interested again."

"And he would be correct," Isabel answered firmly, ignoring her friends' dubious expressions. "Besides that," she continued, "we conversed before dinner, primarily about Salisbury Plain and Stonehenge. Of course, we were not seated together during dinner, though he seemed quite taken with both his companions. I do not think he noticed me across the table once during the meal. He may very well have forgotten me entirely after dinner had Mr. Dunn not accosted him during their gentlemanly port."

Ellen's frown, paired with her sincere eyes, gave Isabel pause and pierced her heart.

"That cannot be true, dearest Isabel. How could he forget you over the course of one dinner when it is obvious that the passage of years did not erase you from his mind?"

Silence fell upon the carriage at Ellen's astute words, disturbed only by the bustle of the street. It was difficult to argue when their most timid member spoke with such quiet conviction.

"Perhaps I should mention…" began Mercy, brows upturned as she looked at Isabel. "I overheard my mother tell a friend during the play at Covent Garden last night that she is eager to invite the newly returned and increasingly popular Earl of Murfield to the musical performance we are hosting next week."

That familiar mixture of emotions, growing in intensity, seized Isabel's chest, both apprehensive and anticipatory and a thousand variations in between. After last night, she should have expected this. With Lord Murfield back amongst the *ton* and reacquainting himself with the finest circles, it was only a matter of time until they began crossing paths, no doubt with greater frequency.

Yet every time she attempted to remind herself that this was a circumstance to be avoided as much as possible, she found she could not construct a truly compelling reason for it. After last night, Isabel should have expected that as well.

"I shall attempt to persuade the viscountess to save Lord Murfield for a different guest list," Mercy continued with a small, understanding smile when Isabel failed to reply.

Isabel shook her head. "No, that is not necessary, but I thank you. I know Lady Eldmar's mind is not liable to change once she is determined on a course of action. Conserve your energy for other ordeals."

Safe in the privacy of her own mind, Isabel remembered how fond Lord Murfield was of music. Music was the perfect marriage of art, science, and history, he had once told her after a beautiful evening at the opera.

She did not wish to deny him any opportunity to enjoy it…or to deny herself the opportunity to discuss the performances and pieces with him.

Their surprisingly lovely conversation last night had felt like the most natural thing in the world. It had ignited such a longing to be near him that Isabel knew she could not maintain her outward denial to her friends for much longer.

"Have any of you decided what you shall play or sing?" she asked, eager for a respite from talk of the earl.

To her relief, the ladies seemed satisfied with the information they had wrested from Isabel and accepted the redirection. As they pondered which pieces would show their skills to the greatest advantage and which duets would complement them best, their ices slowly disappeared and their concerns melted away.

Some unknown amount of time later, Aunt Matilda finished her leisurely walk up and down the block and collected Isabel to return home. She shared the news of Lady Eldmar's plans for a musical performance and the girls' discussions of their participation in the barouche.

No mention of Lord Murfield passed her lips. Until the carriage stopped before the Abbott family's townhouse.

"Lord Murfield?" she whispered, half in disbelief and half in hope. It could not have been possible that she had somehow summoned him with her mind, could it?

At the same moment as Isabel, the gentleman descended from his phaeton farther up the street. He caught sight of her and the dowager countess and brushed at the tuft of bright-red hair that peeked out from beneath the rim of his hat, a leather portfolio tucked under his other arm. Even from here, Isabel could read the nerves in his stuttering movements.

"What a lovely surprise. Lord Murfield has come to call on you again," said Aunt Matilda cheerily. "Now, I must hurry upstairs and speak with your papa before I leave for my dinner. Do invite the earl into the drawing room."

One neat brow raised, Aunt Matilda placed her fingertips at the small of Isabel's back and gave her a gentle push forward.

"Ah, Miss Abbott." Lord Murfield smiled and raised a hand in a hesitant wave.

Isabel went still in that way that only the earl's voice could inspire. Even her curiosity about his sudden appearance at her home was quieted. Perhaps it was simply enough that he was here.

"It appears our timing has begun to fall into step once more," he continued, tipping his hat. When his eyes rose to meet hers again, the hope she saw there—or thought she saw—sent a twinge through her heart.

"Please, come in," Isabel replied as she led them up the steps into the foyer.

She paused halfway to the stairs when she felt Lord Murfield's absence behind her. She looked over her shoulder to find that he had paused in the middle of the foyer, clutching the portfolio against his middle.

"My lord?"

"You were so interested in my travels that I thought I would bring some maps as well as a few of the paintings I made to chronicle the scenery, though of course they are rather crude by comparison despite my improved skill. Still, I thought these might help you get a sense of it all."

He thrust the portfolio, sealed by clasps, out to Isabel. Confused, she glanced from Lord Murfield's offering to his face.

"You may take as long as you like perusing them. Until next time, Miss Abbott."

"Wait!"

Lord Murfield's eyes widened as Isabel crossed the room in a few strides. She gripped one end of the portfolio loosely.

"Stay. Please."

The earl's gaze only grew wider, matching Isabel's own surprise. "I-If you wish…"

In some distant corner of Isabel's mind, a bell of alarm sounded. This was all too familiar. They had done all of this before— the strangely exhilarating uncertainty, the unspoken desire, the longing looks. And they knew where it ended.

The force of Lord Murfield's stare as he waited for her was enough to muffle the alarm. It even softened the edges of painful memories.

"I am sure I shall have a million questions that can only be answered by you, so you may as well stay," she said quietly.

The gentleman's face split into a wide grin, the freest she had seen him since he had come back into her life. It nearly took her breath away. How desperately she had missed that smile that had once graced his handsome features more often than not, especially in her presence.

He slipped the portfolio out of Isabel's hand and offered his elbow. "To the drawing room, then?"

Could it truly hurt, just for one moment, to pretend as though no time had passed? Isabel pondered and savored that question as she took Lord Murfield's arm and ascended the grand staircase by his side.

"Arthur, would you have tea brought to the drawing room?" Isabel asked a passing footman in the hall.

"Lady Ainsworth has already requested a tray for the drawing room, miss. It should be there now."

"Very good." Isabel gestured for the servant to join them in the drawing room and attend to their needs—and to the necessity of some supervision for two young, unmarried people.

She smiled at her lovely aunt's thoughtfulness as Lord Murfield led her in, leaving the door wide open. The earl helped Isabel settle onto the sofa in the middle of the room while sensible Arthur made himself busy at the sideboard with preparing cups of tea and plates of treats for his young mistress and her visitor.

When Lord Murfield turned to take the chair beside her, the memory of their first night as renewed acquaintances flashed through her mind. Isabel did the unthinkable once more.

Her hand shot out and captured Lord Murfield's wrist. The delicate lace pattern of her gloves did nothing to protect her skin from the shock of heat that rushed up her fingertips, up her arm, into her heart.

Lord Murfield's russet-brown eyes, as kind as they were med-itative, glanced from Isabel's hand to her face with a look she could not quite identify.

"Sit beside me," she said, her lips suddenly dry.

She fought the urge to lick them. It was far too unladylike, not to mention the fact that she had dropped her focus to the gentleman's mouth in an attempt to avoid the questions she'd glimpsed in his gaze.

Perhaps that, too, had been a mistake. Lord Murfield's lips looked far softer than hers felt at present.

"It will be more convenient for me to view your materials if you sit beside me, will it not?" Isabel added. Her quiet rationalization sounded rather more yielding than resolute, much like when she had rationalized her reason for asking him to stay.

"Quite right. But…" Lord Murfield nodded and looked down at his hand, still claimed by Isabel's grasp.

For just a moment, she hesitated. It was enough to be noticed by both of them, yet not enough to be remarked upon. Not even when the tips of Isabel's fingers trailed along the back of his hand as she released him. Neither did their eyes break as Lord Murfield sank onto the sofa beside her.

Much too close, that muted voice of reason chimed. When Lord Murfield's leg brushed against Isabel's, her senses had no choice but to desert her. His knuckles whispered across the silver, gossamer fabric covering her knee as he unclasped and flipped open the portfolio, spreading it over both their laps.

Isabel prayed he did not feel the jolt that raced through her body, tingling from the top of her head all the way to her toes. Why should such closeness cause such a reaction? They had been this close before—closer, even.

How could something so simple feel just as intoxicating as it had four years ago, yet comfortably familiar, yet also wonderfully foreign all at once? Isabel could not begin to fathom which thread to follow first, or if she truly wanted to know what awaited her at the end of each.

"Tea, custard tarts, and honey cakes, miss, my lord," announced the footman from halfway across the room, carrying an artfully arrayed silver tray.

Whether he knew it or not, Arthur had afforded Isabel and Lord Murfield the opportunity to compose themselves. At least, Isabel knew she required a moment to remind herself to breathe. Just then, the earl also seemed to realize how much he had encroached upon Isabel's space. He scooted down the sofa, laying out the portfolio between them.

"There, that is better. We will both see more clearly," said Lord Murfield.

Isabel missed the warmth of his closeness immediately, her side exposed, empty.

"Would you like me to have another table brought up so that his lordship might display his documents?" the footman inquired.

"That will not be necessary. Thank you, Arthur."

Unable to remove her gaze from Lord Murfield, Isabel waved a hand in dismissal. The servant bowed and retreated to his post along the wall, poised with hands behind his back.

"You need not remain quite so far, my lord."

A week ago, Isabel would not have believed she would ever say such a thing to the man who had caused her so much heartache. The man himself seemed hardly able to believe it as he awkwardly collected his portfolio once more and slid back toward Isabel, though not quite as close as he had been before. He seemed to think better of it, brows furrowed.

Lord Murfield lowered his head. "Are you certain? I have been so afraid…"

"Afraid of what?" Isabel asked. Guilt pricked at the hidden tenderness in her heart.

He looked up, eyes alight with sincerity.

"I have been terrified of causing you any more discomfort than I already have, and I have feared that your genuine good heart compelled you to accept a truly undesirable position as my friend. Hence why I did not make a greater effort to seek you out sooner."

Isabel smiled. Something inside her felt a little more right than it had before. "I believe I have quite left all that behind—the worst of it, at least."

Surprising her, Lord Murfield exhaled a sigh that sounded to Isabel like relief. His sturdy, broad shoulders drooped ever so slightly. The angles in his face eased into softness.

"You cannot know how much that means to me, as undeserving as I am," he said under his breath.

A muscle in Isabel's neck twitched. Memories prodded at the back of her mind. She did not wish for their conversation to veer any closer to the past than it already had. She wanted to enjoy this moment as something new…a fresh start of sorts. If not, she would be driven mad by this grudge.

"Now, how much longer do you plan to keep me in suspense?" Isabel tapped the leather portfolio.

"Ah, yes, here we are," Lord Murfield said, his smile widening as he extracted the first sheet and brandished it before Isabel.

Despite biting down on her bottom lip and covering her mouth with a hand, Isabel could not silence her giggle at the sight of it. It turned into a true laugh when Lord Murfield pouted.

"I did warn you that my paintings would be crude. You know I have never had much natural talent with art, yet I had no other means of capturing my memories. Alas, if they are so far below your standards, I shall trouble you no further," he half-grumbled, half-teased, rising from his seat.

Isabel could hold it in no longer. Her laugh burst forth as she lurched forward and took hold of his hand once more with both of hers.

"No, stay!"

What followed happened in the blink of an eye and left Isabel breathless. How could she not be when all of a sudden, she found her former suitor's nose a mere hair's breadth from her own, the radiant color of his gaze consuming her entire field of vision?

In Isabel's rare bout of playfulness and thoughtlessness, she had pulled upon him with greater strength than she'd realized. Lord Murfield had lost his balance and they'd toppled gracelessly to the sofa. Isabel's back pressed against the armrest. The earl hovered over her, one hand gripping the carved back of the sofa, the other cradling Isabel's head, lest she bump it against the side table. One knee was propped against the cushion, nearly touching Isabel's hip.

They remained perfectly still for an agonizing, delicious moment. They had been *this* close only once before…the one and only time they had shared a kiss.

Only Isabel's heart retained its freedom of movement. It

thundered and buzzed and danced in that way that she had felt with no one but this man before her.

Perhaps she was mad, for she had no possible way of knowing short of asking aloud, yet she suspected that Lord Murfield's heart experienced much the same. She took the strange, enticing shine in his eyes as they held hers captive—and the fact that he had not yet moved away—as plausible evidence. For now, in this moment, it would do.

"Good heavens, forgive me." Lord Murfield gasped as his senses returned, his entire face flushing the color of his hair. He scrambled up and away from the lady, bumping against the long, low center table behind him before hastily resuming his seat and smoothing down any loose waves against his forehead.

When Isabel righted herself, her attention went straight to the wall on their left. The heart that had been so carefree a beat ago shot into her throat, dread icing her veins. The footman stared straight ahead as if intently studying the view of the brick building through the window across.

"Stay here," she whispered from the corner of her mouth to Lord Murfield, rising swiftly.

"May I be of assistance, miss?" asked Arthur as Isabel approached. His hazel eyes just barely widened when the young lady came within a step of him, betraying his surprise before his professional composure returned.

"Yes, you shall be of immense assistance should you promise to keep what you just witnessed to yourself," Isabel hissed in an urgent whisper. "It truly was nothing but a clumsy mistake. Do you promise?"

Arthur nodded quickly. "You have my word, Miss Abbott. I saw nothing untoward because nothing untoward occurred."

A touch of relief loosened the tension in Isabel's chest. She gave the footman a grateful smile. "Thank you, Arthur."

Isabel returned to the middle of the drawing room, where Lord Murfield waited, and sat back down beside him. "Now, where were we?"

The earl opened his portfolio once more to reveal his water-color Stonehenge. "If you are quite finished ridiculing my earnest effort, I thought I would begin with the treasures in Salisbury Plain since we spent the majority of our time last night discussing it. I also brought maps of the area, of course."

Like before, he slid closer and spread his display across their laps. Isabel gave all her energy to focusing on Lord Murfield's words instead of how close he sat, the entire side of his body brushing against hers, or how lovely it felt to share such peaceful proximity. Eventually, as she relaxed and found herself falling into the wonder of his stories, following along on the maps and artwork he'd brought, a thought almost more alarming than any Isabel had had thus far flitted across her mind.

She blinked hard in an effort to banish that vague wish. To share the mystery of Lady Swan with the earl would have been madness. No doubt he would have been just as fascinated and eager to search for clues and formulate theories...if the letter were not about himself, of course.

Considering how nearly fatal the revelation of Lady Swan's letter had been to Felicity's relationship with her husband, Atticus, Isabel could not risk a similar falling out. Not now. Not when he had only just returned and things between them had finally begun feeling easy...like the old days.

She blinked hard again. What had become of the Isabel who had been sure of being the first one to wave farewell when Lord Murfield disembarked once more?

The earl tapped at a spot on the map, sending the thought scattering from Isabel's mind.

"And here. This would be the exact place one must stand for an optimal view of the sunrise behind the Heel Stone during the summer solstice. It was a thing of miraculous beauty, though I am not sure many would brave the early hour and poor roads to witness it."

He paused, his whole being softening, and chuckled. Isabel watched from the corner of her eye, a quiet awe slowly washing over her.

If Lord Murfield could reflect with such a sweet, glowing fondness upon these difficulties he'd sometimes encountered during his travels—which would have been considered gross inconveniences to many members of the *ton*—then it must have been true.

The earl *loved* this life.

An unwelcome pang struck Isabel somewhere deep in her stomach. After seeing such a look on Lord Murfield's face, how could she wonder why he'd stayed away for so long, or why he'd disappeared in the first place?

Everything about this great country, full of riches to dazzle the eyes and broaden the mind—to say nothing of the bits of the broader world he'd experienced—was far more interesting than Isabel could ever hope to be, no matter her accomplishments or cultivated intellect.

"But thus far," Lord Murfield continued with a sheepish smile that made Isabel ache, once more jarring her away from that melancholy darkness, "if I manage to make it to this point, my audience usually shudders to imagine forcing themselves out of bed at such an unnatural hour. Nor are they inclined to heed my suggestion of forgoing grand events the night prior so as to take advantage of the early morning."

"Please, continue," Isabel urged immediately. "You never need fear offending whatever delicate sensibilities remain to me after making a daily habit of extensive study and practice, remember? I am no stranger to rising with the sun, even after a long night…though I must confess I do not often rise before it."

Without thinking, one of her hands covered his where it rested atop the map, obscuring a swath of Wiltshire.

Why could she not stop reaching for him? Was it because their hands knew each other, could sense the history between them?

"You never need to fear sharing anything with me, remember?" she added, so quietly that if the gentleman had leaned away at that precise moment, he might not have heard. As the silence stretched on, she was not sure she *wanted* him to have heard.

Isabel's heart began beating erratically, fluttering at a dizzying speed. Her senses had been well and truly compromised. This was all too much. *He* was too much.

"It is such relief to know there is still at least one soul in this world with whom that can be true," he whispered. He was so close that his warm breath drifted across Isabel's forehead.

"Whatever happened in the past, that will always be true with me." Isabel's reply had come before she could process the words falling from her lips. Before she could hesitate.

Who was she?

The sweet memories swirling in her mind's eye, the wonder of the present moment, and the glimmer of possibility that awaited on the horizon had neatly tempted her away from the bitter principles she had used to hold him at arm's length.

"Isa—"

"Isabel dearest, who do we have here?"

Panic shot down Isabel's spine like a strike of lightning. The young pair scrambled to their feet and spun around to face the drawing room door. Clutched in both of their hands, Lord Murfield's map of Wiltshire's Salisbury Plain sliced through the air so rapidly that it sounded at risk of tearing.

Isabel's father stood in the doorway, his stout figure taking up most of the space, one hand resting atop his middle. Despite Papa's naturally rosy complexion and generally jovial temperament, Isabel could read the questions in his eyes as they bounced back and forth from his eldest daughter to the man he had once been sure of calling his son-in-law.

"Sister!" called Maria as she poked her head around Papa. Squeezing herself against the frame, the girl weaseled her way into the room. A smile illuminated her delicate features. "Is that a map?" Maria asked with a delighted squeak.

"Maria, mind your manners!" cried Papa as he tried and failed to capture his youngest child, grasping at air as she skipped toward Isabel and her visitor.

With ease and elegance, Lord Murfield lifted a hand to the older gentleman. "Do not fear. I would never fault a fellow lover of cartography for her enthusiasm."

Isabel forced herself to regain her composure, ignoring the sweet scene beside her of the earl dropping to one knee and unfurling the map before dear Maria's sparkling eyes.

"Papa, good afternoon. You recall that Lord Murfield and I shared quite the discussion of his journeys across the United Kingdom. He was so kind as to visit with the most wonderfully detailed maps and paintings of his expeditions over the years and has been transporting me with incredible tales."

She waved one hand toward the map in question, now being diligently prodded and examined by Maria and Lord Murfield, with whom she shared an anxious glance. Why had they been sitting *so* close?

"Of course I recall! He transported me with a fair few tales last night as well." Papa laughed as he took a step into the room, turning his attention to Lord Murfield with a grateful nod. "How good of you to call on us, my lord. I am afraid I must beg your forgiveness, for I must now remind Isabel to ready herself for tonight's play and ensure Maria returns to her governess."

Groaning under her breath, Maria pouted down at the ground, defeated.

"I hope you will allow me to call again soon and peruse my maps with you as well, sir," said Lord Murfield with a relaxed smile, rising to his full height, the very image of a perfect gentleman. Only Isabel could feel the tension radiating from him.

Papa brought his hands together in a resoundingly enthusiastic clap, grinning from ear to ear. "Nothing would bring me greater pleasure, indeed! Alas, it is a terrible shame we shall be obliged to wait until another time."

Lord Murfield offered his regretful agreement and farewells. He spared nothing but the barest glance over his shoulder at Isabel as he quickly collected his things and quit the drawing room. It was enough. For what, Isabel did not have time to wonder.

"Off you must go as well, both of you," said Papa with a chuckle, holding out an arm.

Silently, Isabel obeyed, taking Maria by the hand and hurrying across toward the door. Everything had happened so fast, and now it was...over. It had taken all of an instant for reality to shatter around them once more.

As she passed by Papa with her customary swift peck on his cheek, as well as a one-armed hug about the waist from Maria, Isabel watched her father from the corner of her eye. Apart from his initial reaction of mild surprise, perhaps more so at the presence of *any* guest than of that particular one, nothing seemed amiss in his demeanor.

Until, as Isabel took those first few steps down the hall beside a happily chattering Maria, her continued unease nudged her to look back. This time, her gaze went not to Papa, but to the other man who occupied the room with them. Still stationed along the wall, it was now Papa who whispered in the footman's ear.

Isabel's stomach turned itself into an impossible knot. Of course she trusted Arthur to keep his promise...to the best of his ability. Though she had assumed more and more duties of the mistress of the house since Mama's death, the final word still belonged to Papa. He could compel any of their staff to divulge any information if he saw fit.

Turning on her heel, Isabel spurred herself down the hall to the schoolroom and delivered her sister to the care of a frazzled Miss Oakley, who had just returned from the chamber pot and had been searching for her charge, then went up another flight of stairs to the family wing. The last thing she wanted was to bump into Papa again after all this strangeness.

Isabel breathed a sigh of relief as she reached the security of her quarters. Only then did the knot in her stomach finally begin to ease at the memory of her hand and Lord Murfield's joined together like they had never come apart.

CHAPTER SEVEN

FERVENT CHATTER AND bustling commotion greeted Caleb and Wrighthall as the Eldmars' butler announced them into the music room. Everywhere Caleb's eye turned, something glittered, from the perfectly spherical floral arrangements nestled within tall, porcelain vases—themselves gilded with a keen eye toward moderation between tastefulness and extravagance—to the twinkling chandelier above.

Yet none shone so bright as the young lady who stood at the front of the room near the raised platform, frowning in concentration. The corner of Caleb's mouth tugged up in a smile as he watched her flip through her sheet music. If he'd been a betting man, he would wager that Miss Abbott had prepared pieces for pianoforte, harp, and voice. She had made herself a great proficient at all three.

The smile evaporated in an instant when a man appeared from the corner of Caleb's vision and strode with blond head held high, propelled by self-assurance, straight toward Miss Abbott.

He was too far to hear any of their conversation or attempt the imperfect art of reading their lips. Yet he recognized well enough those civil stances, the chivalrous gesturing on the part of the gentleman, and the cultivated blankness of the lady's expression in response, as well as the protective monitoring of her father and aunt from a safe distance.

"Careful, my friend, or you shall be accused of gawking at

best and glowering at worst," said Caleb's friend to his right. Chuckling, Wrighthall clapped a hand upon his shoulder and squeezed, forcing Caleb to turn. "If you must, you may resume your *observations* after you have dealt with—"

"Lord Murfield, Lord Wrighthall! Welcome to our little evening of musical fun!"

They turned to the overly amiable voice of Viscountess Eldmar. The older woman approached with what struck Caleb as a rather determined smile. Faint shadows cast by the dozens of flickering candles suspended in the air above them deepened the lines around her mouth and at the corners of her eyes in a way that went beyond charm or motherliness.

"How very good of you both to join us," said Lady Eldmar as she paused before the gentlemen and sent a sharp glance at something over her shoulder.

Dutifully, Miss Mercy Reeve slipped out from behind her mother and curtsied to Caleb and Wrighthall. Lady Eldmar placed a dainty hand upon her daughter's shoulder. No, Caleb realized after stealing a closer glance, her hand did not quite make contact with Miss Reeve.

"I hope you remember my youngest child, Mercy. You may not have heard, but her sister, Felicity, has recently been happily settled with a fortuitous match that I myself arranged. She is Mrs. Wheadon now. Surely, our dear Mercy will be following suit very soon!"

"Many congratulations to your family, and all my prayers for your ever-growing joys," Caleb said with a smile. Wrighthall, more distantly connected to the evening's hosts, nodded his agreement.

Seemingly pleased with their simple platitude, the viscountess continued with an increased air of confidence, narrow chin jutted up.

"You have arrived at precisely the right moment for my talented daughter to open the night. Would you not consider that to be fate, Lord Murfield? Ah, Mr. and Mrs. Webb, I was beginning to fear we would be compelled to begin without you!"

With farewells to Caleb and Wrighthall, Lady Eldmar ushered in the newest arrivals. Whether she had forgotten to drag along her daughter or had intentionally left her to converse with two eligible gentlemen, Miss Reeve did not seem to mind. Nor could Caleb blame her when he saw the crimson coloring the poor girl's face.

"I pray you will forgive my mother's...forwardness. She is merely eager to recommend me after orchestrating, in her own eyes, my sister's recent success. I will inform her that she must leave you both be," Miss Reeve said with a sigh.

She glanced about at the various members of the *ton*, who thankfully appeared too distracted with finishing their conversations and refreshments to take heed of the viscountess's desperate indiscretion.

"Surely, she is eager to recommend you because your accomplishments merit it," Caleb offered, more out of a sense of politeness and a desire to spare a young lady from the embarrassment of having an audaciously marriage-minded mother. He recalled, however vaguely, from past conversations with Miss Abbott about her beloved friends and their charming community in Bainbridge, that the Reeve twins had never shared a particularly close or caring bond with their parents.

Miss Reeve gave her a smile that tightened at the corners, perhaps apprehensive. Her eyes darted to Lady Eldmar and followed along for a moment as her mother strode toward the platform.

"I trust you will understand if I do not wish to..."

Caleb shook his head quickly. "Not in the least. I would not leap at the opportunity to court anyone who had harmed one of my friends, either."

The lady's dark eyes widened. "That is not what I—"

"Welcome, beloved friends, to our evening of exquisite musical entertainment!" Lady Eldmar's voice, bordering on shrill, cut easily across the chatter in the room. Miss Reeve excused herself and hurried to the front of the room, sending an apologetic glance over her shoulder.

To Caleb's dismay, their position near the door rendered it impossible to secure seats with a prominent view of Miss Abbott. He and Wrighthall were compelled to take chairs in the second-to-last row toward the end. The principal performers, Miss Abbott included, occupied the row nearest the small stage.

Just as Caleb quietly exhaled his disappointment at being unable to see even the back of her head around all the others, a sliver of space cleared. His heart jumped. Miss Abbott's stare arrested him even from across a room full of people.

Why she should be staring at him, Caleb could not guess. Since his visit with his maps and paintings almost a week and a half past, they had only encountered each other once in passing at Covent Garden during intermission and could only speak of the drama that had unfolded thus far on the stage.

Then again, perhaps there was nothing to be said of the drama that had almost swept them away, more than once, in the drawing room. Perhaps the drama existed entirely within Caleb's mind. If so, why was Miss Abbott still looking at him with that inscrutable intensity?

"What have you done to her?" Wrighthall whispered in Caleb's ear, a perplexed brow arched high. "I thought you said you appeared to be making progress when you last spoke properly."

"We were. We are," Caleb insisted under his breath as Miss Reeve took her place at the pianoforte. "But the drawing room business... What if she has found it to be unsavory upon reflection?"

Wrighthall almost rolled his eyes. "The pair of you spend too much time in reflection. Don't you think it rather makes a mess of things that should be quite simple?"

"Ah, and are you an expert on such matters?" Caleb retorted in a hiss.

The first chords of Miss Reeve's piece resounded through the music room, silencing the two gentlemen's childish bickering. Caleb could only wrinkle his nose at his friend as he shrugged a shoulder in feigned ignorance of the accusatory question.

As the performances continued—including one on the pianoforte by Miss Abbott, one he'd heard her play before—Caleb felt his mind being drawn away from Wrighthall's playful, truthful jab. He gave himself to making mental notes on the pieces chosen and which he liked best should he have the opportunity to share them with Miss Abbott later. As with all else, sharing discussions of music with her was nothing short of a perfect union between insightful and delightful.

Caleb sat up straighter when he noticed Miss Abbott rising again and watched as she joined Miss Gardiner on the platform for the first duet. The latter perched atop the pianoforte bench while the former approached the edge of the stage.

Assured of his safety in the back of the room, he allowed himself a real smile as Miss Abbott signaled for her accompanist to begin with an expression so gentle, it pierced Caleb's heart even from this distance. When Miss Gardiner did not begin, her hands hovering over the keys, eyes wide, Miss Abbott gave another nod and a subtle motion to inhale.

It was a small, natural thing for Miss Abbott to do, yet it made a world of difference in her friend's confidence. Miss Gardiner played in a manner as tender as her nature and no less skillfully than any of the others who had displayed their talents thus far.

Yet it was not until Miss Abbott began to sing that time stopped for Caleb. Her voice, a crystal clear, resonant soprano, soared through the room, then faded to a delicate, precisely controlled whisper, then leapt triumphantly. She infused every word, every breath, every expression with a feeling that elevated Caleb's spirits to a degree no music had ever done before. The muscles in his face went lax with wonder.

So much had changed. Miss Abbott, already so perfect in his memory, had grown more beautiful and more kind-hearted, had further sharpened her mind and refined her accomplishments.

Only she could make it possible to improve upon perfection.

Caleb continued to stare as the duet finished to polite applause, Miss Abbott's face aglow with graceful pride at a successful performance. He barely registered the tap on his shoulder.

"Move along, my friend, if you do not wish to develop a cramp in your legs," said Wrighthall with another, more insistent tap.

Blinking as if waking from a mystical dream, Caleb realized that an intermission must have been called during his daze. Half the guests had already found their feet, eager to stretch or fetch refreshments, Wrighthall included.

"Ah, here comes Miss Abbott," the baron added, chuckling as Caleb jumped up, suddenly wide awake.

"Lord Murfield, Lord Wrighthall, good evening. I trust you are enjoying the entertainment?" asked Miss Abbott as she approached their end of the row along the wall.

"Very much so, indeed. A job well done to both you and Miss Gardiner," Wrighthall answered warmly. "But I shall leave Murfield to tell you more. I am in great need of a cup of tea before we resume."

With that, Wrighthall left Caleb and Miss Abbott alone—at least as alone as they could be in a room full of people. In fact, in the corner as they were, Caleb hardly noticed anyone else and hardly cared if anyone noticed them.

"What say you, Lord Murfield? Do you agree with Lord Wrighthall?"

Her eyelashes fluttered, chin lifting up ever so slightly in anticipation of his answer. The chandelier above cast shades upon her green eyes that even the great masters could never hope to preserve in oils or watercolor. Her pale skin and round features caught their golden light and subtle shadows, reflecting them back. Warmth flooded Caleb's chest.

"Not entirely."

Miss Abbott's neat brows twitched. "I am grieved to hear you say so, particularly for Ellen. She was plagued by dreadful nerves and practiced tirelessly—"

Caleb chuckled as that warmth wrapped around his entire being. The lady fell silent.

"I only meant his praise was not strong enough. It was the most sublime, moving performance I have had the privilege of witnessing, Miss Abbott. You sang wonderfully."

She tore her defiant gaze away. "Now you are just being hyperbolic, sir. Besides—"

"Miss Gardiner played wonderfully as well. I commend her dedication and bravery, truly," Caleb said quickly. Miss Abbott's eyes snapped up to meet his once more, perhaps surprised that he had read her thoughts.

"That is very kind of you. Will you allow me to repeat your words to her? We all experience anxiety on such occasions, but it drives poor Ellen mad. She needs encouragement more than most."

Caleb nodded, unable to speak for the awe gripping his soul. For the first time, he did not care what his smile might reveal. He would not deny it if pressed. He loved the way she loved her friends.

"So..." Miss Abbott continued slowly, breathing a little quicker, as if flustered. "You really think we...I did well?"

Caleb nodded again. This time, the words came easily. "Without a doubt. I meant every word. You have clearly continued to practice and it does you credit—unlike my laughable painting skills. I have always greatly admired your dedication, you know."

Pride returned to her gaze, a smile widening across her face. "I have always appreciated your admiration. Not everyone notices the effort I put forth, though of course I do not do it for praise."

"It is not a fault to desire praise when one is as deserving of it as you are," Caleb replied quietly and honestly.

Did his eyes deceive him or had a tinge of color risen to the lady's cheeks? She glanced down. "Thank you. Perhaps I might return your kindness by inviting you to join me at Vauxhall at the end of the week?"

For a strange moment, Caleb wondered if something had gone dreadfully wrong. Did his ears now deceive him as well?

"Truly?" was all he could muster, his throat suddenly dry, as if only her answer would quench the thirst.

Miss Abbott raised her head once more, a little higher this time. "There is some reading material I have been enjoying of late that I wish to discuss with you. None of my other friends or family take the same interest in sermons, no matter how much I try to convince them that not all such writings are as dreadful as Fordyce's."

"Of course—"

Before Caleb could finish his response, a silky, pink blur raced past them toward the door. Without a word, Caleb and Miss Abbott exchanged concerned glances and followed together as Miss Clara quit the music room. Thinking quickly, Miss Abbott managed to catch her aunt's eye as they reached the door and waved for her to accompany them into the dimly lit hall.

Miss Clara spun around with a piercing squeak when she heard footsteps behind her.

"Isabel, is that you? Oh, thank goodness, dear Isabel!"

Even the few candles illuminating the empty hall could not hide the tears spilling down the younger girl's face. Her lower lip trembled with the effort of keeping her sobs contained as she nearly threw herself into Miss Abbott's arms. Caleb and Lady Ainsworth lingered a few steps back, watching with growing alarm.

"Whatever is the matter, darling?" Miss Abbott inquired in a soothing tone.

She wrapped an arm around her friend's shoulders and guided her farther into the privacy of the shadows just as Miss Gardiner appeared in the doorway, a hand pressed to her chest. In a rare, unladylike display, she ran to her sister and Miss Abbott.

"It is the most terrible news! I just heard from Mama!" Miss Gardiner cried. She took Miss Clara in her arms and, with some difficulty, tucked the slightly taller girl's head against her bosom.

"Heard what?" Miss Abbott demanded.

"While we were waiting for the music to resume, I made mention to Nicholas that last night, I had a dream about Dreamer, of all things. And he thought it a fine opportunity to inform me that he'd sold my Dreamer last week!"

Red splotches erupted across Miss Clara's face. Her small hands gripped Miss Abbott's arms in desperation. "Without warning, without allowing me a chance to say goodbye! And Ellen's Priscilla now has a buyer as well. What sort of brother sells his sisters' most beloved horses without so much as a hint of remorse? Only the cruelest, most wretched sort!"

"Oh, Clara…"

Without another word, Miss Abbott pulled both her friends into a comforting embrace. Silently, Miss Gardiner rubbed small circles against Miss Clara's back, her expression pale and forlorn.

"You poor, poor creature," Miss Abbott whispered against Miss Clara's hair, eyes closed and mouth a pained frown. "And poor Dreamer, too. I am sure your faithful mare will miss you immensely. None of you deserve such treatment. It is cruel and wretched, indeed."

Caleb's hands tightened into fists at his sides. Lady Ainsworth lowered her head and shook it.

The cold, angry undertone in Miss Abbott's voice would have made Caleb shudder had it not been so justified. There was only one reason for a man to resort to selling his family's belongings, especially those of innocent sisters in his safe-keeping. Caleb did not recall many specific details about the Gardiner family, yet he was sure he would remember any indication of such a severity in the brother's spending habits.

Still, issues in the ledgers could be kept from the light for years, decades even, before the cracks began to reveal themselves. It was the tragic fate that increased every family's dread with the arrival of each new generation. There was always more to protect—and lose.

A footman from within the music room was soon dispatched to inform them of the music's imminent continuation, which the dowager countess intercepted. As she offered a vague explanation and apologies to the hostess with promises of their swift return, Miss Abbott continued to hold the distressed girl, swiping at her tears with a handkerchief. Assured of her sister's care, Miss Gardiner excused herself to assist their sniffling mother, who appeared almost as distressed as her younger daughter.

"There, there," Miss Abbott cooed patiently. "How I desperately wish I could return Dreamer to you—or better yet, return to an earlier point in time and somehow prevent Mr. Gardiner from doing such a thing by *any* means necessary…"

She paused, hooking a finger under Miss Clara's chin. The other lady gave a watery smile and huffed out a chuckle between gulping whimpers. Caleb almost shuddered again.

Mr. Gardiner had no clue how grateful he should have been that no one had yet discovered the means to traverse time, for Caleb believed Miss Abbott would very well keep her word.

"But since I doubt either of those courses are possible, I promise to aid you, and Ellen of course, in any way that may be useful. Even if it is merely to be your personal handkerchief attendant."

Miss Clara giggled as Miss Abbott dutifully dabbed at more tears with a smile that spoke of nothing but her love and concern for her friend. Soon, Miss Clara grew somber again and let her head fall heavily onto her friend's palm, pressing her cheek into the smooth fabric of the handkerchief.

"I love Dreamer, Isabel. How am I to bear it? How am I to return to Bainbridge and look out my window at the pasture, knowing she will not be there? How am I ever to have any enjoyment in riding again, knowing there is no other horse more suited to me?"

"Dear, sweet Clara," Miss Abbott murmured, pulling the

other lady into her arms once more. "You are never to forget, Miss Clara Gardiner, that I shall always be here to laugh with you during the good days and lift you up during the bad. The same is true of the other girls. Whatever you bear, you do not bear it alone. Let that be of some comfort to you. Though it is never easy to hear and even harder to accept, time must do all the rest. Your only responsibility now, my dear, is to allow it." Miss Abbott whispered so quietly, Caleb almost did not hear.

Part of him felt he should not have. Yet the greater part of him somehow *knew* that he'd needed to hear it. Almost as if her words had been meant for him.

"Thank you, Isabel, truly," Miss Clara replied, sniffling. "Can you believe it? All these theatrics for a horse! You must think me terribly silly."

Miss Abbott chuckled and shook her head. "Not in the least. You love deeply and feel loss deeply. There is never any shame in that. And you already ask so little of anyone, always searching for ways to make those around you happier by any margin, no matter how small, because to you, it is always worth it. It pains me to see any hardship befall you."

After a few more sniffles and calm reassurances from Miss Abbott, Miss Clara declared herself recovered enough to return to the music room. Caleb and Miss Abbott followed more slowly, watching the normally sprightly girl retreat down the hall with head lowered, Lady Ainsworth behind them.

"You spoke very kindly and wisely," he said, breaking the melancholy silence.

"I worry for them both," Miss Abbott admitted without removing her eyes from the music room door.

"Do you know his club? Perhaps I might have a chat with that gentleman…"

Miss Abbott turned sharply to look at Caleb. Her brows shot up in surprise before lowering back to the realm of reality.

"That is extremely gallant of you, my lord, and it will bring some cheer to Clara to hear of it, but you know it would not be seemly. Though I wish that were not the case, in this instance."

"I must insist that you inform me immediately if there is any way I might be of service to those ladies."

Miss Abbott gave a small smile, fond and bittersweet, and nodded.

"You did well by your friend. I admire you for it."

"Thank you, but it is only what I would do for anyone I love," Miss Abbott answered quietly, pausing in the doorway.

Her gaze remained fixed on Caleb, steady. He'd seen this look before. He would know it anywhere by the wave of bliss that drowned his heart.

Love.

Could it be? Could there possibly be hope for the dream Caleb had buried alongside his brother? Or had he merely slipped into the dream again, that torturous one where Caleb and Isabel had never needed to become Lord Murfield and Miss Abbott?

Miss Abbott blinked, slowly, her long lashes catching the light of the chandelier. For some reason, in Caleb's dreams, she never blinked.

She was real. This was real. It was becoming more real with every passing moment, sending them spinning toward a horizon they could not see beyond.

Lady Ainsworth's light cough reminded them of where they were. Luckily, an unfamiliar young lady on the harp kept the audience's focus away from the trio as they took seats in the back of the room.

The feeling of lightness that had been filling Caleb's limbs did not dissipate, exactly, as if disappointed, but instead paused, waiting. All at once, he was certain. The time had come to tell her why he had really left. He would tell her everything from now on, if he might be granted the privilege.

Yes, Caleb did wish to tell her, but not tonight. She had given over enough of her evening to supporting Miss Clara and deserved to enjoy the rest of it. As they listened to the angelic melody of the harp, his ease and optimism increased.

Miss Abbott had proved beyond a shadow of a doubt tonight what Caleb should have always known. He need never have suffered through his grief and unexpected responsibilities alone. She would not have been ashamed of him. And she deserved the truth.

Perhaps, despite his best attempts to avoid it, sharing the most sorrowful secret in Caleb's heart was the way for them to bridge the gap he had forced between them once and for all.

CHAPTER EIGHT

EXHILARATION AND BLAZING lamplight flooded every corner of Isabel's mind as she disembarked from the boat on the bank outside Vauxhall Gardens, her hand secure in Papa's. No matter how many times she visited this place, its wonder never diminished.

"There we are, careful now," said Papa as he guided Isabel over the small, slippery pebbles of the bank and up onto the walkway.

She was grateful for his stability, and Lewis's presence at her back. Isabel could not help craning her neck to admire the colorful lanterns that lined the path toward the gate and the playfully twinkling stars above. Without her family to direct her, Isabel might have wandered all the way to the Dark Walk in her haze of astonishment.

"I do not see them," Papa grumbled quietly as a group of recent arrivals surging toward Vauxhall absorbed them into their ranks.

The misgivings in his tone finally tore Isabel's attention away from the lights that promised even more fantastical sights within. She glanced up at Papa from her peripheral vision and then cast her gaze about the growing gathering.

"He will be here," Isabel answered. "I asked him to join us, so he will be here. I am certain of it."

It was Papa's turn to look at her curiously. Isabel did not

flinch. For the first time, she *was* certain. She did not know how or why precisely, only that every recent meeting with Lord Murfield had revealed the thoughtfulness and sweetness that had captured her heart the first time.

As if in answer to a prayer Isabel did not realize she'd made, their steadily moving crowd slowed just before the gate. There along the wall stood Lord Murfield and Lord Wrighthall with a small group of gentlemen huddled around them.

The earl seemed to notice her in the same moment. No wave of relief came, only a feeling of rightness that had eluded her since they'd last met at the night of the musical performances. Isabel had missed him.

The light from the colored lamp hanging above them bathed Lord Murfield's smile in a soft, lavender shadow. The earl and the baron made their farewells to their other companions.

"Good evening Messrs. Abbott, Miss Abbott," the two gentlemen said as they wove their way into the eager throng at the gate.

"Lord Murfield. Lord Wrighthall," said Papa. "My, what a handsome, little party we make! Shall we enjoy our mystical evening?" No trace of his earlier hesitance remained.

Lord Wrighthall valiantly stepped forward between Papa and Lewis and effortlessly engaged them both in conversation. Instinctively, the earl offered his arm to Isabel and she accepted just as naturally.

"Do my eyes deceive me or does your popularity increase every time I see you these days?" Isabel asked. She smiled up at Lord Murfield, only to find him already smiling down at her, radiant in the bold, golden glow of the lanterns surrounding them.

"I suppose so, though I still cannot fathom why," Lord Murfield replied with a chuckle. "Eventually, they will realize that I truly have not done anything so extraordinary. Not as extraordinary as the time we went to Astley's and that trick rider was thrown from his horse and flew into our seats—"

"And you caught the poor fellow before he could rush our entire section!" Isabel's giggle, quickly covered by a gloved hand, was drowned out by sighs of awe and whispers of wonder.

They passed through the gates of the proprietor's house into Vauxhall Gardens. Isabel and Lord Murfield added their own exclamations, their heads turning this way and that, eyes bulging in an effort to absorb the magnificent beauty surrounding them.

What seemed like thousands upon thousands of lamps of all colors, hung from posts and upon carved arches, blazed with an intensity that rivaled all the stars in the black, velvet sky above. They stretched on and spread out as far as the eye could see, lighting every path, pavilion, and grove, enticing stunned visitors with promises of even grander spectacles than they had yet seen. Music from the centrally located orchestra filled the cool, night air with an effervescent spirit.

Yet none of it affected Isabel quite so much as the look of enchantment that illuminated Lord Murfield from within. She had yet to see him look quite so peaceful and untroubled since his return. The skin around his eyes and between his brows was smooth. His firm cheeks and jaw held no tension. Perfect lips parted in silent wonder and then began forming shapes, words.

"Miss Abbott?"

The real world, as unreal as it seemed in a place such as Vauxhall, rushed back to Isabel. She cleared her throat. "Pardon me, I must have been caught up in the spectacle. Though I am sure they have made many improvements in the years since your last visit."

"I only asked if you might like to promenade nearer the orchestra. Your family and my friend appear eager to see and hear more."

"Of course, certainly," Isabel answered, praying that her heart would soon return to a normal rhythm.

Lord Murfield had not seemed to read anything in Isabel's unintentional stare, perhaps too overcome by the general splendor, but what if he had? She might have given herself away entirely in just that look.

Signaling Isabel's acquiescence to the others, they moved deeper into Vauxhall down the main walk, lined with trees, trimmed shrubs, and more lamps than any one person could ever hope to see in a single lifetime. In the distance rose the orchestra box, designed to resemble a towering temple of extravagance, from which spilled the most rousing music from the best performers in all of London.

"Lord Murfield," Isabel said after a few moments of walking and gazing and greeting other patrons in the wake of Papa, Lewis, and Lord Wrighthall.

She disappeared into her reticule. With one hand, Isabel brandished her small notebook. The earl paused, a smile of recognition spreading across his face. How many hours had they spent discussing her carefully curated quotes and formulating insightful additions of their own in pages just like these?

"Here you are. I have copied the passages that struck my particular interest—and my accompanying thoughts on them, naturally—from that collection of sermons by Sedgewick I mentioned recently. I think you shall find that I am correct in my assessment that this author, though sadly unknown by most, is far better than that odious Fordyce. This will offer an introduction to his ideas, and mine, but I hope you will secure your own volume so we might discuss them at greater length."

As she set the small book in Lord Murfield's hand, he glowed not with lamplight and starlight, but with pride…in Isabel. His fingers wrapped around the smooth leather, a soft smile on his lips.

"I recall you were quite fond of my old green one, so I had another made in its likeness just for this purpose," Isabel added, her enthusiasm tempered by delightful, intoxicating anticipation. Leaning closer, she bumped his upper arm with her shoulder, both playful and comfortable.

"Might we discuss it now?"

Isabel tilted her head back to peer up at Lord Murfield. They passed under a lamp of blue glass that revealed the curious blaze in his eyes.

"How do you propose we do that? You have not read the sermons themselves, let alone my little scribblings."

The earl chuckled and, almost absentmindedly, settled his other hand atop hers where it rested in the crook of his elbow. Their relaxed footsteps crunched softly against the fine, gravel path as it wound around a corner. Surely, to any of these passersby—if any of them cared to notice with so much else to captivate them—Isabel and Lord Murfield must have looked like any smitten couple with the altar in mind.

"That hardly matters, not to me. I would listen to you speak on subjects innumerable, no matter how unknown to me, for however long you had breath. And, as always, I would do my best to keep pace with you. Besides, I am most interested to hear *your* opinions."

Isabel's smile grew wider, almost a grin. At times like this, she wished that she need not be compelled to restrain her happy expressions or laughter, but that was the way of this outer world. In their old inner world, whatever moments of relative privacy they'd been able to snatch, Lord Murfield had made it clear that Isabel was never to dull herself in thought or action in his presence.

Yet, despite the dozens of people wandering about, including Isabel's father and brother and Lord Murfield's companion, the mystical atmosphere of the gardens—and perhaps their own immersion in their growing closeness—created a strange sense of insulation, enclosing them in a bubble of their own making.

"Well, firstly," Isabel said with her usual deep, purposeful inhale that made Lord Murfield smile with a familiar adoration, "I think it is a terrible shame that Sedgewick is not more widely circulated than Fordyce."

The delightful music resounding from the orchestra faded into the background of Isabel's words. Lord Murfield hummed thoughtfully, pinching his chin with the fingers of his free hand.

Delicate wings fluttered in her stomach at that look she had loved so very much.

"And why is that? I daresay this Sedgewick fellow must possess quite a wise mind if you believe him to be superior to the much-admired Fordyce."

Isabel nodded, unable to suppress her grin any longer, unconcerned by negative reactions from onlookers. No one she had met before or since Lord Murfield knew precisely what to ask and say to ignite the excitement of her intellect.

"I will concede that Fordyce has his merits and expresses some sensible ideas that are worth sharing and possibly applying in some degree to one's own life."

"But?" Lord Murfield's curious smile radiated brighter than the dozens of lights overhanging the walkway.

"But I favor Sedgewick's sermons for their emphasis on the necessity for greater allowances between differences in individuals, especially for women," Isabel replied in a rush, her passion building under his encouraging gaze.

"For example," she continued, "you recall that Fordyce champions ideals such as humility, meekness, and obedience as commendable, indeed necessary, feminine traits in every woman.

"According to him, they not only provide her with the means of recommending herself to potential suitors—thus bringing her closer to fulfilling the essential duty for which she was created—but they protect her from bringing irreparable shame to her family. He himself admits that the world is quick to forgive innumerable sins of the son while casting out the daughter at the first mistake."

"I do recall. And I recall that you have never thought that particularly fair. Nor have I. Does Sedgewick agree with us?"

Isabel could feel her eyes shining with the joy in her heart. She had not realized until now just how terribly she'd missed this…missed him.

"You have an excellent memory, my lord."

"I could never forget anything involving you."

The air fled from Isabel's lungs in a sharp exhale, a muscle in her neck tightening. Lord Murfield's gaze went straight to it. She felt vulnerable, exposed, and secure all at once.

This felt like before, during their first Season…the timidity and excitement of being seen by another in a way no one else had quite done before. If this truly was a repetition of that time, that meant they were only one step away from falling… Could she truly allow herself to take that step with *this* man?

"Sedgewick falls closer in line with my own views on the subject, yes," Isabel said under her breath.

Their group had come all the way around to approach the front of the orchestra now, forcing Lord Murfield to lower his head closer to hers to hear properly. The tip of his nose nearly brushed the soft skin of her temple. Isabel made no attempt to pull away.

"Of course, I do not claim that such qualities are without their place in the characters of *every* person, man or woman. In fact, it is my belief—and Sedgewick's—that we could all benefit from them, but not to such a degree that they completely eradicate one's natural disposition and inclinations—and foster this unjust divide between the sexes that indulges one while punishing the other."

The music crescendoed as they stopped at the outskirts of the lawn that stretched before the orchestra, populated with a crowd in raptures. A shadow touched the earl's features.

"It would be a terrible shame indeed if you had not been allowed to flourish as your truest self. I agree with you both that the *ton* could do with far less judgment overall. A happier, easier world it would be if there existed a greater harmony between the unyielding ideals of conduct books and the reality of the varied and fallible human nature we all possess."

As the larger group next to theirs pushed toward the front, Isabel had no choice but to tuck herself deeper into Lord Murfield's side. Yet even after they had passed, she remained so close, he felt almost a part of Isabel herself.

The rest of the world continued to spin and dance and make music around the pair while they remained blissfully oblivious.

"I quite missed your eloquence in these engaging conversations," she whispered without looking at him. "No one is quite so willing to delve into a problem as you are, and delve into the new ones we find—or make—along the way."

Lord Murfield did not respond right away. He did not shrink away from Isabel's gaze when she finally looked up at him, as he'd sometimes done at odd moments here and there, as if embarrassed or uncertain. For some reason, Isabel sensed that the earl wanted her eyes on him when he spoke again.

"I am of the same mind about you, Miss Abbott. No other soul on this Earth, of whom I have met more than enough, has had any real hope of comparing. I...I wish I had not stayed away so long."

"Why did you?"

There came the question Isabel knew must one day be answered. Her spirit would never truly be at rest without it. She swallowed the sudden burning sensation in her throat. Was she finally ready to understand why he'd delayed his promise to return to her by four years?

For the first time that evening, Lord Murfield's focus left Isabel and darted to the trio standing several paces ahead of them, just visible between other members of the entranced audience. They all seemed distracted enough with admiration of the music and lights to not mind whatever revelation was about to illuminate the darkest times of Isabel's life.

Lord Murfield did not continue right away, his eyes falling to the grass beneath their feet, shoulders dropping slightly. He took a long, deep inhale. Whether steeling himself or planning what he would say next, Isabel could not tell.

Sympathy for things she did not yet understand tugged hard at her heart. Isabel brought her free hand up to join the other on Lord Murfield's arm and squeezed them both.

"When you are ready."

He looked at her with the saddest smile Isabel had ever seen. It nearly cracked her heart in two.

"I am ready now. Firstly, I must apologize once again for my disappearance and the grief it caused. I know that I behaved despicably toward you, regardless of my own situation…"

A large cloud passed overhead, plunging the crowd into even darker shadows and timing well with the dramatic swell of the strings. The crack in Isabel's heart deepened. It was the same one that had been put there by this very man.

She did not like to revisit those days, not even all these years later. Yet it had become clearer to her as more time had passed and as their friendship had deepened that they would never be able to move forward without finally facing it. Isabel tightened her fingers around Lord Murfield's arm once more, this time to brace herself.

"Your situation?" she prodded gently.

Lord Murfield's sharp jaw tightened. "Of course you remember that I claimed to be called away on some minor business and would rejoin you in London in a few days, but I failed to do so or send word as to why. Then, several months later, you heard about my brother's unexpected death. But what I believe no one knows, what I have kept from almost everyone, is that my disappearance and Daniel's passing were, in fact, quite related."

Confusion temporarily replaced Isabel's melancholy, her heart stopping. How had she never considered that these two terrible events may have been linked despite the conflicting chronology?

"At the time, I thought it would be easiest to allow everyone—including you—to think that I had simply lost interest and gone to live a life of travel, and had only stopped to bury my brother and manage the most necessary of my duties as the new earl before departing again. I did travel, of course, but only after…"

Isabel's stomach hollowed, her eyes widening as she struggled to comprehend Lord Murfield's words. Suddenly, the fanciful melodies from the orchestra sounded discordant and full of dread.

"Do you mean…good heavens, do you mean…?"

He lowered his head and nodded slowly. Locks that fell in gentle waves swept across his forehead and temples.

"Yes, toward the end of that Season, I'd decided to seek Daniel's advice and encouragement on a particular matter. As my elder brother and only remaining family, I looked to him for everything. It was my greatest desire not only to receive his enthusiastic support, but to share this moment of joy with him. I'd planned to return to surprise you with his blessing and my proposal.

"When I arrived, I discovered that my joys were not to be. My brother had remained home to begin plans for renovations to many of Osborne Park's rooms, you see, or so I had thought. But in truth, he'd hoped that remaining in the comfort of our estate in Berkshire would cure him of his strange illness…an illness I'd known nothing about until it was too late."

Lord Murfield paused and swallowed. Tears filled Isabel's eyes and weighed heavy in her chest.

"Daniel had not wanted to worry me, especially because I had only been properly introduced to the excitement of London Society the year before…and because I had been writing to him about the fantastically intelligent and beautiful young lady, who, for reasons I still cannot fathom, had deigned to lower herself from the skies and grace me with her presence."

Despite the terrible pain gripping Isabel's chest as she listened to her friend's heartrending story and recalled her own experience with grief, she could not help the small smile that flitted across her lips. She hadn't known that Lord Murfield had written to his brother about her. She hadn't known any of this, which contributed to her misery in no small part. No one should have suffered such a shock alone.

"How absolutely dreadful," she whispered through the emotion lodged in her throat, just barely audible over the orchestra.

"It was," Lord Murfield answered, his voice hoarse. "It was

the most dreadful thing I have ever experienced, watching the brother who had been my idol, the very definition of vitality, waste away before my eyes in a matter of days. Of course, by the time I'd learned the worst of it, most of him was already gone. Skin and bones, kept alive only by the strength of his spirit…"

Isabel squeezed her eyes shut, a tear slipping down her cheek. She had no doubt that she would be haunted in much the same way if she had been subjected to witnessing her beloved mother's painful last breaths, watching the life leave her eyes.

"Caleb, I am so, so sorry. All this time, I made a villain of you in my mind to soothe my own pain while you endured an agony I cannot begin to imagine, with no one to care for you as you cared for your brother."

The earl's eyes widened. Isabel's breath caught in her throat. He held both Isabel's hands in his in a grip that was both desperate yet loose at the same time, as if he never wished to release her again but would do so without hesitation at the earliest signal. His lovely eyes, such a mesmerizing, rich brown, fixed her to her spot. Not that Isabel had much of an inclination to go anywhere again unless he was by her side.

"Sister! Hurry along or you shall miss the fireworks!"

"Yes, Murfield, were you not telling me on our way how eager you were to see the fireworks at Vauxhall again?"

The calls from Lewis and Lord Wrighthall dragged the pair out of their reverie and away from each other. Whether intentionally or not, the two younger gentlemen, standing shoulder to shoulder, blocked Papa from a view Isabel knew would bring him some discomfort.

"Yes, yes, the fireworks," the earl agreed, looping Isabel's arm around his once more.

Did she imagine the heat simmering between them everywhere their figures made contact or brushed against each other? Or did she merely feel the heat of embarrassment at having used a gentleman's Christian name, even if she'd done the same in the past?

As their group and many other guests shifted their spots on the lawn for more advantageous views of the spectacle, Isabel pondered the strange sensations within. She knew she should have been embarrassed by such a blunder, yet for some reason, she could not bring herself to regret it.

With one hand on Papa's shoulder and the other on Lewis's, Lord Wrighthall situated them in the upper corner of the lawn, facing the Grand South Walk. Many already looked to the skies in anticipation. Not the Earl of Murfield.

"You called me…"

A boom erupted overhead. The ground shook. Fiery, golden sparkles crackled in an impossible burst of light before fading back into the velvet, black sky. Gasps of awe surrounded them.

A rush of boldness and another stunning spray of red fireworks swept Isabel up in the moment. Though she had not intentionally used his Christian name, at present, she could see no harm in taking advantage of the opportunity.

"Perhaps it is time I was Isabel to you once more."

He responded with something that was not quite a smile but still conveyed a depth of contentment that Isabel felt mirrored within. "Nothing would bring me greater happiness, Isabel."

She inhaled and exhaled slowly as swirls of green danced amongst the stars and her name danced on his gravelly voice. It sounded natural, like it had always been and would always be his to use.

"I am glad I can offer some measure of happiness, after all you have endured." Isabel prayed he could feel the earnestness in her words.

"You have brought me some of the only happiness I have known since Daniel left this world."

"I wish I could have been with you all those years ago. I would not have been so cold to you if you had explained."

Caleb tightened his grip.

"You did not know any better, and that is entirely my fault. You had every right to vilify me and I do not blame you in the least. It is I who must beg forgiveness, continually, until I can be sure to have driven out all the pain I caused and replaced it with the happiness you deserve. I would beg with gladness, daily if need be."

Isabel slowly shook her head and squeezed back. "Thank you for saying so, and thank you for sharing this with me."

"Thank you for waiting so patiently, too patiently, to hear it."

Another magical explosion of fireworks inspired shrieks of delight from the audience. For all Isabel and Caleb knew, the world may have been falling to pieces around them.

Or maybe it was finally falling back into place.

CHAPTER NINE

THE PROMISE OF summer enveloped Isabel in welcoming warmth and vibrant color as she descended from the coach. Lush leaves on trees and hedges burst with the jolly green that heralded blooms in every shade, swaying in the breeze. Hyde Park in the quiet morning was sublime. Isabel had never felt so…right.

"What a perfect day for Lord Murfield to have invited us to promenade," said Aunt Matilda as she linked arms with Isabel and opened a parasol over them both. "What do you think, Isabel? Has the earl written to Mother Nature herself and requested this beautiful afternoon sky and these sweet songbirds for us?"

Thinking quickly, Isabel turned to look over her shoulder and waved at Papa to hurry along, grateful for the protection her bonnet afforded her. They passed under the iron archway that led into the bustling park.

"I am afraid that has more to do with luck, dear aunt, though I am sure if Lord Murfield could have contrived it by some means, he would have."

"He always seemed to me to be such a thoughtful gentleman," Aunt Matilda mused.

Isabel only nodded in reply, quickly engaging Papa in light-hearted conversation when he came upon her other side and looped her free arm around his. They walked slowly down one of many gravel paths that carved elegantly through Hyde Park's expansive lawns, nodding at familiar faces. Isabel's heart hummed. Caleb was here, waiting for her.

They were so close, Isabel could nearly taste it, and it tasted very much like her memory of Caleb's lips…sweet and full of adoration, with an intriguing pinch of salt that had left her longing for more.

Around the next corner, partially obscured by tall, thin hedges, their group nearly ran into the very gentleman. Isabel spied his shining, red hair first and pulled Papa and Aunt Matilda to a hasty stop before a collision, dust and loose rocks kicking up. Her eyes widened as he turned with the most endearingly perplexed expression. It melted into recognition when his gaze found hers, forsaking all others.

"You are here," said Caleb quietly, almost in awe, before remembering his other guests. "You are all here! Lady Ainsworth, Mr. Abbott, Miss Abbott. I am so thrilled you could join me, though I am sure we will miss the younger Mr. Abbott."

Lord Wrighthall appeared from behind the earl and gave him a light bump with his elbow. "We understand completely, of course. We would never deny a young man the opportunity to cheer alongside his friends during a bout of boxing."

Papa chuckled and nodded, though his polite smile did not reach his eyes. "Alas, such entertainments are too exciting to capture my interest now. I find that a promenade out of doors is just the thing these days."

Almost as if they had orchestrated their movements, Caleb and the baron stepped forward at the same time, the former before Isabel and the latter before Aunt Matilda. The gentlemen offered their arms and the ladies accepted.

"Lady Ainsworth, did I not happen to see you entering Somerset House last week just as I was leaving? Have you been to Somerset House recently, Mr. Abbott? I daresay you must visit before the Season's end and witness the latest wonders of art on display for yourself!"

Lord Wrighthall, now in possession of Aunt Matilda's parasol, began the flow of inquiries and chatter with an expert level of gentlemanly civility, turning his head back and forth between his companions, keeping them equally distracted from the pair following slowly behind them.

"Good afternoon, Isabel. I trust you have been well since Vauxhall?"

Caleb began quietly, slowly, relaxed, as if time had never been of any concern and could never affect them. Despite the natural beauty around them as far as the eye could see, the earl seemed content to ignore it all. His gaze never left Isabel's face, his feet seeming to carry him forward of their own accord.

Isabel tightened her grip on his arm just a touch in an attempt to keep her own feet on the earth. His proximity did not help matters, however. Nor did the sweet longing in his eyes every time she glanced up at him. Nor did her heart's inability to settle on a rhythm, whether swift and dizzying or a deep thundering.

"I have been very well, indeed. And you, Caleb?"

No one had ever had the power to muddle her mind like this before—or since. When they had first met and these feelings had begun to stir inside Isabel, they'd frightened her. They'd been foreign and intangible, resistant to her normal modes of inward investigation…until, one day, without warning or reason, nothing had made more sense than the rightness of her and him together.

This time, she was not frightened.

The earl stopped, forcing Isabel to do the same. Luckily, no one had been walking too closely behind them. In fact, Isabel hardly noticed any of the other ladies and gentlemen—couples, friends, families all seemingly enjoying this fine, late spring day without a care in the world.

"I have been far, far better these past several weeks with you than in…I almost do not wish to admit," Caleb finally answered with a small smile.

"I feel exactly the same," said Isabel in a whisper she knew only he would hear.

A light cough sounded from somewhere behind them. They started and whirled around to find another young couple, most likely a few years older than them and married, watching from a few paces away with knowing smiles.

"Pardon us," said the unfamiliar man lightly, gesturing at the walkway that Isabel and Caleb had accidentally claimed as their own.

Sputtering apologies and glowing red, they scurried off to the edge of the path. The lady, dressed in a becoming amethyst that would have been considered too mature for an unwed girl, made sure to catch Isabel's eye as they passed.

"Many blessings upon you dears," she said under her breath before looking up at the man who was no doubt her husband with a contentment in her expression that Isabel knew well. Soon they turned down a fork that led toward one of the park exits.

Caleb and Isabel caught their breath and resumed their walk with lengthened strides, Isabel's skirts fluttering about her ankles, to decrease the distance between them and the rest of their group. Alarm whispered in the back of her mind when she realized that Papa had been subtly eyeing them over his shoulder while chatting with Aunt Matilda and Lord Wrighthall, though for how long, she could not guess.

"May I ask you something?" Isabel began, eager to ignore her father's apparent curiosity about her conversation with the earl.

"Anything. Always."

"About what you told me at Vauxhall? I do not wish to bring up any—"

"Anything. Always."

Caleb's emphatic statement sent Isabel's heart into the most splendid flutter she had ever felt, even during their first courtship. Why did this seem so different than before? So much more...secure?

"Did you truly think I would have been happier without you, hardships and all?"

There was no accusation or anger in Isabel's tone. Despite her best intentions and staunchest objections, she had given up her resentment for the most part some time ago. With this new information connecting the missing links that had plagued Isabel's mind these past four years, any last vestiges of bitterness slipped away on the breeze.

"I know now that is not the case," Caleb replied with a heavy sigh. "Especially after witnessing how tenderly and willingly you cared for Miss Clara that night. But, of course, I should have known the entire time and allowed myself to rely upon you instead of thinking I could avoid dimming your light with my grief by hiding amongst the country's relics.

"By the time enough of my senses had returned, too long had passed for me to feel that I had any hope of regaining your trust, at least without revealing the nature of my brother's death. I'd also heard from Wrighthall of your plan to secure a match of material comfort instead of companionship. I was sure I would be hearing further news of your nuptials with every passing day."

Isabel raised a brow and tilted her head to obtain a better view of the gentleman. "Did you ask your friend to spy on me?"

The tips of Caleb's ears reddened, matching his hair. "Not to spy, no. Merely to keep an eye turned toward you, lest you fall into the hands of some unscrupulous fellow."

"And what would you have done, had I seemed in danger of such a fate?"

"I am glad it does not seem we shall have to find out," he answered quietly. A tinge of hope laced through his low voice.

As much as Isabel's heart longed to pursue that thought to its long-awaited, inevitable conclusion, her mind would not release a crucial detail of Caleb's earlier words.

"If I may ask another question, why did you wish to hide your brother's illness?"

The earl's eyes flew up to the others walking ahead of them, only a few feet now from the Serpentine and the busy bridge that allowed park visitors safe passage over it. He swallowed.

"It was not my wish, but Daniel's. In some strange way, I

thought I was honoring him by observing it to the strictest degree possible. Or perhaps that was merely another excuse. My brother took great pride in his spirit and sense of adventure, you see."

A memory from her first Season flashed through Isabel's mind. Eyes on the path before them, she nodded somberly.

"I recall you telling me about his perilous carriage chase to hunt some ruffian who had snatched a loaf of bread straight from the hands of a poor villager. That must have been the night of the Georges' ball, when the elderly gentleman standing beside you lost several of his false teeth on a candied plum."

Caleb laughed quietly, a little lightness returning to his countenance. "I certainly recall *that*. And the numerous ladies who fainted from the sight of it. But it heartens me to know that you remember such things about my brother. He would have been very pleased, no doubt.

"The first thing he said to me upon my arrival, after apologizing and explaining, was that I must never tell anyone the true cause of his demise. He said he'd been planning to write to me soon and had even concocted a story of a harrowing accident for me to share when the time came, though he did give me permission to confide in Wrighthall. No matter how I tried to convince him otherwise, my poor brother was terrified that the world would reduce the vibrancy of his life to his sickly final moments."

Caleb paused, lifting a hand to rub his rigid jawline. Isabel nodded her understanding.

"I truly am glad you did not endure it all entirely alone. And that you were able to spend that precious time with your beloved brother."

Caleb pursed his lips and let out a slow exhale.

"In fact, Daniel may very well have lost his chance to tell me himself had his estate manager not finally convinced him after months that I needed to be prepared for what lay ahead and the role I would play in it. I only happened to return home as Daniel was finally finding the words, as he'd said.

"But we became so overwhelmed with the increasing needs of his declining state and the arrangements to be made…and it felt a little wrong, to speak of falling in love and beginning a new life under such circumstances. I never told him why I'd returned, nor did he ask. We were simply glad to be brought together before the end, whatever the reason."

"My goodness," was all Isabel could muster for several long moments. "That must have been a terrible burden to bear—not only your loss, but all the responsibilities you never expected to gain."

They stepped from the gravel path onto the smooth surface of the bridge. Papa, Aunt Matilda, and Lord Wrighthall tarried in the middle, peering out over the stonework wall at the crystalline water below.

"In my head and in my heart, I still think of him as the true Lord Murfield," Caleb confessed. He frowned, brows knit low over his long nose. "I fear he would have been disgusted by and ashamed of his successor."

Isabel's head turned sharply. She stared at the gentleman's profile, strong in the golden sunlight and sweet in the cool shadows. A perfect balance. But even perfection must bow in the face of life's tragedies.

"Now that is truly the most foolish thing I have ever heard from you."

Caleb halted once more. Luckily this time, they had veered naturally closer to the bridge wall, where they could remain out of the way of other passersby.

"P-Pardon?"

"I did not have the privilege of knowing your Daniel in this life, but if he loved you as much as you love him, I can imagine no world in which he would not agree with me. *Truly* think of who your brother was. Do you still believe that he would be anything less than immensely proud of you?"

Her heart shot into her throat at the sight of Caleb's misty eyes. In her peripheral vision, Isabel noticed their party continuing toward the other end of the bridge. Without thinking, she slid her hand from its comfortable position on his arm down to his wrist.

"I thought I could never imagine a world without my brother breathing and running and laughing in it," he whispered. "And now here I am, living it. How can you be so certain that he is not looking down on me and weeping for the failure I am?"

"Caleb."

His name escaped her lips, almost as a plea. Emotion welled inside Isabel once more. She allowed her fingers to slip a little lower and intertwine loosely with his.

"You could not be any further from a failure, Caleb, I promise you. I know you have your regrets and mistakes, but they do not add up to the sum of a failure. If you cannot accept such words on your brother's behalf, accept them on mine.

"I certainly do not blame you for how your grief manifested now that I understand your circumstances. I know what it is to lose someone long before you are ready, on what should be the happiest occasion of one's life, like an engagement, or the birth of a child."

"Your mama. I remember how fondly you always spoke of her."

"I have had more time, and more help, to move me along in the world when I could not fathom growing up in this complex, terrifying place without my mother. Though I was just a girl, I recall all manner of strange thoughts and behaviors during our mourning period that my governess eventually convinced me to give up. Besides, in the end…"

"In the end?" Caleb's thumb brushed over the light, silk fabric of her gloves.

"You returned." Isabel sighed, strangely content despite this melancholy air. "You returned, and everything was made right."

The gentleman's gaze dropped to Isabel's mouth. "You truly believe so?"

"I know so. I have all the evidence here."

She tightened her hand around his, keeping their infraction hidden between their bodies and the bridge wall. It was not without its risks, considering anyone down below lounging on the lawn or paddling their boat along the river's undemanding current might catch a glimpse at the right angle. Isabel could not care any less.

"Do you remember the first time we walked across this bridge?"

"I could never forget, even if I tried," Caleb answered under his breath. The heaviness that had weighed down his handsome features softened and smoothed. "Just down there, we met for the very first time at a picnic. Never had I seen such mesmerizing, green eyes—nor have I since."

"Never had I seen such blinding-red hair." Isabel giggled, covering her mouth with her free hand.

Every feeling of that first moment swept through her as if it were happening all over again.

The strange tingling when their gazes had met over their cups of tea, the way her ears had perked up every time she'd heard him say anything of interest, the bubbles under the surface of her skin when their knuckles had brushed as they'd reached for the same pastry.

It rushed back to Isabel in exquisite clarity and threatened to send her floating into the sky, just as she had nearly done that day.

"And up here," continued Caleb as he led them toward the top of the bridge, "in an effort to keep the dwindling conversation flowing and prevent the party from breaking up, Wrighthall asked everyone to share their favorite philosophers."

"Quite a few of the others thought it a dreadfully dull question not deserving of serious consideration. But we both answered at the very same time—"

"Wordsworth," they said in unison.

Isabel's smile grew wider to match Caleb's grin. "We spent the rest of the walk marveling at our shared fascination with both his unique, rustic artistry as a poet and his philosophy of the common human experiences we all share, regardless of birth."

"A swan."

Every muscle in Isabel froze. "What did you say?"

Caleb narrowed his eyes at her and pointed over the edge of the bridge. "Look, a swan on the water. Forgive me. I thought you liked them."

Isabel swallowed. "They are beautiful creatures, yes, with an air of mystery about them…"

A frown soon appeared below the furrowed brows and narrowed eyes. "Does something trouble you? About…swans?"

Stomach twisting, Isabel threw a glance over her shoulder to be sure the others, now at the opposite foot of the bridge, were well enough out of earshot. The words hummed on the tip of her tongue.

She had wanted to share it with him for so long. Now seemed as good a time as any, with both of them standing on this familiar precipice once more.

But what would her former suitor—possibly current suitor—make of these supposed strings that had pulled them together this Season in the form of a cleverly written anonymous letter? It had not been a success initially for Felicity last autumn, whose revelation of Lady Swan's letter had caused a nearly irreparable rift between her and her new husband.

"Isabel, you may tell me anything, remember? You will never have any judgment from me."

The tenderness in his voice and eyes sent a wonderful shiver down her spine. She felt the truth of his words somewhere deep in her soul, in the same place that she hoped her words had reached him earlier. If he could be truthful with her, then she owed him the same.

"I suppose, in all your adventures, you have never encountered anyone called Lady Swan, have you?"

"Lady Swan?" Caleb paused, one brow furrowing while the other arched. "Not exactly. A Lady Swanley sounds familiar. I might have crossed paths with a Mr. Swanford once or twice, but there was no Mrs. Swanford that I knew of."

"You would not know if any of them happens to be a talented writer…or matchmaker?"

"Matchmaker, you say?"

The concern in his expression swiftly transformed into intrigue. One brow arched so high, it almost disappeared under his fringe, his mouth pulling to one side. Isabel could not help chuckling at that darling look. She prayed that from now on, she might have occasion to see it daily.

"I suppose I shall start from the beginning."

"That is usually the most sensible place to start, yes."

Isabel shot him a teasing glare that coincided well with the firm step down from bridge to earth. "Continue like that and I think I might keep the secret to myself, after all."

"You wound me!" Caleb laughed and clutched his chest in exaggerated pain.

The sound was brighter and warmer and more essential to Isabel's life than the sun above. Soon, her laugh, not quite as bold, joined his as she explained the mystery of Lady Swan, starting with Lydia's letter last Season.

"And the next letter arrived at the start of this Season…" She trailed off, a hint of nerves returning.

"Fascinating!" cried the earl.

Isabel could almost see the thoughts spinning through his mind in his blazing eyes. So, too, she assumed, could a handful of nearby strollers and picnickers, who looked askance at the young couple before quickly turning their attention away from the frivolity.

She regretted not lengthening her summary by just a few moments when she saw the trio before them disappear into a tunnel of trees that covered a portion of the walkway. Caleb's enthusiasm would have been better received in that relative privacy.

"Was it you who received the next letter?" he asked, the

words spilling over themselves.

It was Isabel's turn to look askance at Caleb. "Yes. That does not disturb you at all?"

He did not answer right away, not until they had entered the tunnel and the rest of their group had exited ahead. He paused, lingering in the deepest shadows in the middle.

Speckles of light dancing on his hair and skin, he maneuvered Isabel to stand before him and grasped her arms above the elbows, his hot palms on her bare skin.

"Why should it disturb me when it seems clearer than ever that Lady Swan, whoever she really is, is correct?"

Every muscle in Isabel froze, this time in the most exquisite way.

She was weightless, timeless. Everything was still but for the steady beating of her heart as it fell into time with the pulse in Caleb's hands—irrefutable, irrevocable proof of his feelings for her.

"I have felt the pull toward you since the moment I left your side, like the tides must always reach for the moon, no matter how far she is. If it is the ocean's fate to follow the moon's gravity, how could I have thought I would be able to return to London, to be in the same rooms as you, and remain unaltered?

"You have changed me, Isabel, in all the best ways. You have done more good in the way of healing my heart than I have any right to claim, but I am eternally grateful for it all the same. I never could stop loving you."

"Caleb," Isabel whispered with what little breath remained in her body. Her hands rose of their own accord and settled upon his broad chest, bringing herself a little deeper into his arms.

"I thought I had been successful in my efforts to stop loving you. When Lady Swan's letter arrived, it seemed the most absurd, unimaginable thing to me. But if she is the expert...I suppose it cannot be such a terrible idea."

"I have certainly had worse." The gentleman's quiet sigh of contentment was warm and delicate against Isabel's skin.

Her eyes eased closed, almost as if she were falling asleep.

Was that not precisely what falling in love was like—closing one's eyes in bed to the comfortable and ordinary, and opening them in dreams to a world of fantastical color and sublime happiness?

But this was not a dream.

Caleb's lips on hers, smooth, gentle, urgent, had never felt more real. She inhaled his orange and sandalwood scent, absorbed the sensation of every nuanced movement of his mouth, his hands still gripping her arms as if he clung to life itself.

None of this could have been replicated in any form of imagination.

Yet, in much the same way as dreams, the moment lasted an eternity and was over in a flash. Isabel blinked up at Caleb and saw her heart mirrored in his serene expression. Somehow, this kiss had been even better than their first. It had nearly written over that swift peck, stolen in the corner of a dimly lit foyer after a long night of dancing, in her memory.

"Ah, here they are! I told you they had not fallen far behind."

Isabel and Caleb nearly threw each other to opposite walls of the tree tunnel in their haste to create the illusion of propriety. Aunt Matilda, shaded by her parasol, appeared at the other end.

"Have we fallen behind? Goodness, it seems we spent more time enjoying this cool shade than we realized, my lord," Isabel lied with a strained chuckle.

"It does seem rather tempting, understandably," said Aunt Matilda.

The dowager countess's calm smile did not exactly dispel the panic currently flooding her niece. It was the glint in Aunt Matilda's eyes that told Isabel she would later be pressed to give some explanation.

Still, she offered a silent prayer of immense gratitude that Aunt Matilda had been the one to nearly catch them—and in such a public place, too! Even in the late morning, when most of the *ton* still slept away the previous night's entertainment, the risk had been significant. Surely, almost anyone else would have leapt at the chance to do their duty and bring shame and ruination to Isabel and everyone who had the misfortune of being associated with her.

"I am afraid that would be the fault of Lord Murfield," added Lord Wrighthall from somewhere behind Aunt Matilda, mostly blocked from view by her parasol. "My friend can be a dreadfully slow walker for a fellow with such respectable legs. I admire Miss Abbott's patience in indulging him."

Returning themselves to normalcy as quickly as possible, Caleb and Isabel linked arms again and hurried to join Aunt Matilda at the tunnel exit. Isabel fought to keep from scrunching her face against the swell of sunlight that burned her eyes, even with the protection of her bonnet, as they emerged. When she managed to open them fully again, she found that the others had resumed their conversation, not much farther ahead this time.

She also found Caleb, the man she had loved once and would love forever, already grinning at her. Unspoken promises shone in his stunning eyes. There was no regret. The power of the kiss that had reunited them had completely erased the shock and fear of potential discovery, as if such concerns had never existed.

Isabel could hardly begin to fathom what had possessed them to do such a thing…other than an accumulation of years of love that had had nowhere to go. It would be stayed no longer when its home was finally in sight once more.

CHAPTER TEN

THE CORNER OF Caleb's mouth tugged down as he flicked open his pocket watch. He glanced at the door and sank further back into his chair, newspaper spread over his knee.

Wrighthall was nearly half an hour late for their meeting at White's—most likely through no fault of his own. No doubt, his mother was employing every technique at her disposal to keep her son engaged—and get her son engaged—at the luncheon she'd scheduled for the first half of the young baron's afternoon.

When Caleb peered over the top of his newspaper at the other end of the dimly lit room, he prayed the Dowager Lady Wrighthall would soon relinquish his dear friend from her grasp. Unease made Caleb's muscles tense at the curious looks he had been receiving from the handful of gentlemen who had arrived several minutes ago. As it was, Wrighthall was already in danger of making them late for their visit to the Royal Academy at Somerset House with a few other acquaintances Caleb had lately been renewing.

Attempting to sink lower in his chair, Caleb realized too late the mistake he had made in acknowledging the other men's presence with his glance. The small group lowered their heads together in a swift discussion. Caleb did not like the look of it. As inconspicuously as possible, he signaled to the nearest footman and whispered for his carriage to be brought round in preparation of the hasty exit he anticipated.

A moment later, two gentlemen emerged, either chosen or volunteered. They crossed the comfortable room, weaving around plush chairs of dark leather and luxurious velvet arrayed in such a way as to give the appearance of casualness and camaraderie.

"Lord Murfield, I thought I'd heard you were a member at White's. What a delight to finally have you back among us," said the first gentleman, the shorter of the two.

"Lord Blackmore, Mr. Perry, a pleasure," said Caleb as they settled into the chairs opposite him, grateful that he had managed to recognize their faces and match them to names, though only just.

"I am afraid we have made you a little uneasy with our staring," began Mr. Perry. "Several of us have heard so much about the famed Earl of Murfield since your return that we have been quite eager to cross paths with you here, where we might converse at greater length and detail." He attempted a smile but could not manage to hold the expression while swiping at the brown fringe that swooped into his eyes.

Caleb attempted a smile of his own. "You flatter me, sirs. In fact, I could not be more gratified by the *ton*'s attentions to me this Season. I am sure no one could hope to receive a better welcome home."

Viscount Blackmore and Mr. Perry, a future baronet, exchanged a look of approval, despite Caleb's care to avoid further mention of whatever conversation they sought. He had an inkling he already knew the topic on their minds.

"We hear you will soon be leaving London again. At the start of next month, is it?" asked Lord Blackmore, scratching at a scruffy, blond sideburn.

A request to know where such strange information had come from sprang to Caleb's lips just as the memory struck him.

How could he have been such a blockhead? Or perhaps he had not been a blockhead so much as a happy fool in love, blind to all other considerations. And, apparently, to the plans he himself had made after Isabel's initially disdainful reaction to his presence.

"That was my plan, yes," Caleb replied.

How could he have forgotten that he had already mentioned his arrangements to Wrighthall and a handful of other men to stay at an unoccupied converted abbey in Derbyshire? How could he have forgotten that he was scheduled to depart in two weeks' time?

It had seemed like a sensible plan before…before his heart had hopelessly entangled itself with Isabel's once more. Only this time, the bonds that bound them together felt tighter and stronger than before. They must have been, after all they had weathered.

Mr. Perry leaned forward and planted his elbows atop his knees. "And what of this expedition?"

"'Expedition'?"

The other two gentlemen shared another look and Caleb got the distinct impression that they thought him coy for some strange reason. The impression only deepened when Lord Blackmore copied his friend's pose. Caleb leaned back ever so slightly, feeling as though he were being brought into a regrettable confidence.

"We understand your reticence perfectly well, of course. If word spread to too many of such a glorious adventure with you at the helm, you could never hope to accommodate all who seek to take advantage of your extensive knowledge of all the most unique sights to see right here in our very own home. No doubt you would find your own enjoyment of your travels much decreased if such were the case." The viscount paused and looked quickly over his shoulder. "But, should you have any inclination to take on a few more fine fellows, I am sure any or all of us would make agreeable additions to your party."

Caleb bit the inside of his cheek to keep from shaking his head in disbelief. Never would he have expected his travel tales to create such a stir of interest, not only in the stories themselves, but in his supposed expertise. He had certainly not positioned himself as an authority or guide with any sort of intention.

"Alas, at present, I have no schemes for any expeditions," Caleb replied after taking a breath to compose himself.

Lord Blackmore blinked and Mr. Perry pursed his lips.

"Will you make a scheme now?" the latter inquired with a touch more force. "Even those among us who often visit the distant estates of friends cannot claim such extensive knowledge on these locations, particularly the rare ones. We should like to know all there is to know about them before everyone else."

"Again, you flatter me, but as it appears these plans have developed without my knowledge, I am afraid they must unfortunately proceed without my involvement."

"But you have been showing maps to others, have you not?" rebutted Lord Blackmore. "I heard someone say that Mr. Lewis Abbott said you brought maps from your journeys to their townhouse. We were under the impression that the purpose was to include his domestic grand tour in your next voyage."

"Heavens, is that the time?" Caleb rose quickly to his feet, the legs of his chair scraping against the wood floor. "If you will excuse me, I must be on my way to Somerset House. When Lord Wrighthall arrives, would you be so kind as to inform him that I've gone ahead to wait with the others?"

He did not give Lord Blackmore, Mr. Perry, their friends, or anyone else in the room an opportunity to respond. Caleb quit the club with such haste that he nearly cleared the pavement between White's and his phaeton in one long stride. Gently flicking the reins, Caleb silently congratulated himself on his quick thinking to prepare his vehicle of escape just prior to their ambush.

Upon arriving at his destination, Caleb found a bustling Somerset House—a palatial and resplendent home for exquisite paintings and sculptures numbering above a thousand, with what looked to be as many glimmering eyes admiring them. He took his time wandering about the Great Room as he awaited his friend and searched for the others they were to meet, craning his neck to view the less-valuable oil paintings that had been skied.

Caleb had his head tilted almost all the way back for a better look at what he considered to be a very fine pastoral landscape when something familiar in his peripheral vision drew his attention. Isabel's father, walking alongside another older gentleman, had just gone through to the adjoining gallery of watercolors.

A quick sweep of the rest of the room, great indeed and brimming with members of the *ton*, yielded no result of the lady herself. Caleb's pulse quickened. When else would he have the opportunity to ask for Isabel's hand without her nearby or making up some obvious contrivance for a private audience with her father?

Isabel had already received enough terrible surprises from Caleb. This surprise would be welcome, joyous, and answered with a resounding positive. His heart leapt at the thought of it, as if it could reach through time to the future and bring that long-awaited moment to him now.

After working his way through the Great Room's crowd, Caleb was relieved to find that Mr. Abbott and his companion had not gone much further. They lingered at one of the tall columns interspersed throughout the room to display smaller works, their backs to the door.

Nerves made mince of Caleb's stomach as he approached from around another column, palms uncomfortably slick.

"But that Lord Murfield…"

He froze, mouth already open in greeting. The tone of Mr. Abbott's voice did not inspire confidence.

"You mean the one who courted your daughter some years ago? Not his elder brother?" asked Mr. Abbott's friend.

"Yes, the new Lord Murfield."

"I am not as convinced, Abbott. As far as I have seen and heard, he is a perfectly pleasant young man. And by your own admission, he seems to have renewed favor with Miss Abbott. Is it not possible that she's forgiven him and they have made amends?"

Caleb had never uttered prayers quicker in his life—one in thanks of whoever that other man was, the other in the hopes that Mr. Abbott would at least see enough in his friend's suggestions to give some consideration. His hasty prayers died on his lips with Mr. Abbott's next words.

"You do not understand, Hawkins," he continued in a low whisper, weariness softening the anger in his voice. "You did not see the damage he left in his wake. You did not hear night after night of uncertain weeping, which became night after night of devastated weeping when she realized he would not return.

"He broke my girl's heart. What kind of father would I be if I were not at least a little wary of having him in such close proximity again? If I am not mistaken, I am beginning to suspect—fear—that it is happening again. Or will happen again if he does manage to win her heart this time. I know it is possible that his intentions may be strong and true at present, but so I thought once before. How can I be sure now?"

Caleb stumbled back, reeling, his skin stinging as if he had been slapped. But it was well-deserved—on that, he and Mr. Abbott could agree.

"I suppose, when you phrase it like that, I would feel the same if it were my child. That odd thing of his disappearance was such a shame. Will you oppose them if they wish to marry?"

Another step and Caleb's back bumped against the corner of the column behind him.

"That is a difficult question… I fear I will make her miserable if I do, and I fear she will be made miserable if I do not."

Steadying himself, Caleb spun on his heel and rushed through the thankfully smaller and less popular watercolor room with head lowered. His heartbeat hammered in his ears with every swift footfall and drowned out the thoughtful murmurs of the other Royal Academy visitors as he mindlessly wove through them and out into the mostly empty hall.

As soon as he was assured of being alone, Caleb went completely still. The scorch of mortification and self-loathing that had propelled him through the galleries went out in an instant, doused in the coldly realistic view of someone who clearly loved Isabel and wanted the best for her as much as Caleb did.

A single line from Lady Swan's letter, recited word for word from Isabel's memory, rushed to the front of his mind.

"Past pains may lead to a lifetime of joy when two broken hearts heal as one."

It clashed with Mr. Abbott's criticism, stealing the air from his lungs. Caleb's back thudded softly against the wall behind him. He shook his head slowly. It was impossible to reconcile.

How could Lady Swan imply that someone who had hurt Isabel so deeply could be the very same one to heal her? The longer Caleb leaned against the wall, unable to care who happened to stumble upon him in this state, the more Mr. Abbott's position made perfect sense.

If Caleb were truly the right man for Isabel, the one worthy of her beautiful smiles and sparkling conversation and warmhearted care, he would not have acted so thoughtlessly back then. He would have been worthy of her from the beginning.

What had Caleb done with the intervening years but find every way possible to repress his feelings? He certainly had not made much progress toward his own healing, as any rational, mature creature must have done. Not nearly enough, at any rate, to spare Isabel the burden of witnessing his heart's slow recovery if they did join their lives together.

Even if he tried to convince her that it was his duty to finally meditate on the pain of losing his brother and mire through the many complex emotions such introspection would naturally produce, Caleb knew Isabel. He knew her compassionate nature would drive her to give as much of herself as possible to indulging Caleb's gloomy moods and piteous moping.

He exhaled sharply and let his head hang between his shoulders. Mr. Abbott had seen that fact clear as day. It was Caleb who had allowed himself to be blinded to one profound flaw by yet another: selfishness.

And, he must admit, the sheer happiness and love overflowing from him these past few weeks in particular had certainly done wonders to maintain the illusion. He'd had no right to interfere in Isabel's life after leaving her to rebuild it alone simply because the comfort of her presence naturally soothed away the walls around his heart.

"S-Sir? May I assist you? Are you unwell?"

Listlessly, Caleb half-raised his head to find a disconcerted servant, under the employ of Somerset House, watching him from a few yards down the hall bearing a stack of informational pamphlets. Lingering here would not do him much good, Caleb concluded, pushing himself off the wall.

"Thank you, but no. I shall manage."

Though he did not look entirely convinced, the man nodded and continued on his mission, leaving Caleb to the solitude of the hallway once more, but only for a moment. The door to the Great Room swung open.

"Lord Murfield, is that you? What a treat it is to see you here."

Hastily tugging his vest and lapels smooth, Caleb turned to greet Isabel's father.

"The treat is all mine, Mr. Abbott," he said in a rush, fighting his own grimace.

The older gentleman raised a brow of wiry, graying hair but spared Caleb any remarks on his nonsensical wording. He gestured to the lanky man standing nearly a head taller to his right and made the necessary introductions with Mr. Hawkins.

"Have you met with Isabel downstairs in the sculpture room? I am sure she will be happy to see you, as always. If you will excuse us."

Did Caleb only imagine the hint of disapproval he'd sensed in Mr. Abbott's voice and gaze because of what he'd overheard? Real or perceived, it did not change what both men now knew to be true.

What right did Caleb—who'd been so eager to revisit a joyful, uncomplicated past—have to allow his troubles to pollute the happiness Isabel deserved for the remainder of her days?

CHAPTER ELEVEN

"How they manage to find the most fascinating sculptures, from old and new masters alike, to display every year here, I cannot imagine," said Aunt Matilda with a wistful sigh. She turned her head this way and that to take in one last look of the sculpture room.

Isabel paused at the doorway and swept her gaze over the towering marvels of marble, some older than she could fathom. No Season was complete without at least one visit to the Royal Academy. In fact, she would have come once a week if her schedule would have allowed—and if she could have successfully prevailed upon her friends and family to accompany her that often.

The corner of Isabel's mouth twitched up, a pleasant contentment filling her chest. Now she had one person she knew who would gladly join her at Somerset House whenever she wished. Not only that, but he would derive just as much enjoyment out of absorbing every detail of a painting for hours and then spending several more hours ruminating aloud with each other about the skill of the artist as well as the work's thematic elements.

In that way, Isabel and Caleb had always been of one mind. Now, after all these years, against all odds, they had become one heart. Soon, she prayed, they would be made one officially, before the eyes of the loved ones who remained on this earth and those who gave their blessings from above.

They would kiss again on that day. And every day after. How would Isabel survive it? Her lips still stung, in the most heavenly way, since their last kiss at Hyde Park.

"Has something caught your fancy, dearest?"

Isabel started at the dowager countess's question. "Pardon?"

Giggling quietly at her niece's recent tendency toward distraction—which she no doubt knew had something to do with a certain earl—Aunt Matilda tilted her head toward the sculpture room.

"You are wearing quite the pensive expression. Do you wish to have another look at any particular sculpture? We do have a little time, I am sure, before your papa comes searching for us. Or perhaps your mind was turned to something—someone—else entirely? By the name of—"

"Lord Murfield?"

That name, a menace to Isabel mere weeks ago, now set her alight at even a nearly inaudible mention. Unconsciously, she turned in the direction of the voice that had spoken it.

"Yes, as a matter of fact, there is just one thing I wish to view again. I shall return in a moment."

Isabel wasted no time in waiting for a reply of permission from her aunt. Lifting her skirts ever so slightly to make way for the swiftness of her steps, Isabel crossed to a section of busts raised high on majestic pedestals. Her heart skipped when she spied a sliver of Lord Wrighthall between two sculptures.

If he was here, every possibility existed that Caleb would also be somewhere inside the grand building. What a miracle it would be to find him here! Now every meeting with him, whether planned and eagerly anticipated or by chance, felt like a miracle to Isabel.

"—a few friends have been increasing their visits to White's in the hopes of catching Lord Murfield so we can finally have more information about this trip he is leading. But perhaps his closest friend is the next-best resource to the man himself, eh?"

She stopped mid-step. Her knees nearly gave way under her. Thinking as quickly as she was able, Isabel hid herself behind the nearest statue, a great Grecian thing, and put her back to the handful of gentlemen, ears burning and lungs frozen.

"Leading?" Lord Wrighthall repeated.

The lilt of confusion in his voice brought no comfort to Isabel. She squeezed her hands around each other in an effort to keep the rest of her from crumbling, at least until she could do so without fear for her dignity and reputation.

"It is true that Murfield's travels have generated an astonishing amount of interest in his old circles, and the new ones eager to learn of him," continued Lord Wrighthall.

"And with good reason, if I may say so without sounding too much like a biased old friend. I had the privilege of joining him a number of times, though never for very long, per his preference. The earl truly was a fount of knowledge on every area and the little-known treasures within."

"Surely, he must be ready to share that knowledge with the rest of us!" cried another man, unfamiliar to Isabel. "Why else make his return now and tempt us with all his accounts?"

"Indeed, I daresay Lord Murfield could make himself quite the leading authority in the eyes of us gentlemen who desire to discover the secrets of our mother country for ourselves—"

"Without suffering any of the nuisances involved in delivering those secrets to you," interrupted Lord Wrighthall with an edge of sharpness.

Somehow, despite the panic rising like a boiling ocean inside her, Isabel could appreciate the gentleman's caution on behalf of his friend. But when they all spoke about all this with such certainty…

"So, tell us what you know, my lord, we beg you. We do not wish to miss out on what sounds to be an exhilarating opportunity," said the first man to broach the subject. Isabel listened with bated breath.

The baron gave a chuckle that Isabel wanted to believe

sounded like waning patience yet may just as well have been frustration with his own apparent ignorance.

"Forgive me, good sirs, but I am afraid I must confess that the only plan of which I am aware is his trip to study an old abbey in Derbyshire when the Season is finished. He should be somewhere here, though I have yet to locate him, if you would like to inquire directly. Although now that I think of it, there may be changes to those plans, though he has not told me of such…"

"But you do not think he has any inclination to bring companions this time?"

Isabel did not hear the answer to that question. She had heard quite enough. More than enough. It had been too much.

Besides, would the answer change anything?

Keeping her gaze to the floor, Isabel rushed back through the sculpture room toward the door where Aunt Matilda watched her hasty approach with growing alarm. The right answer from the right person could change everything. That much she knew. She also knew why the events of the past had come to pass as they had. If she could only find Caleb and ask—

"Isabel, wait."

She froze just as she reached her hands out for her aunt. A strong though not cruel grip took her by the shoulder and turned her.

"But, Papa, if I could have just another moment to—"

"No," he snipped. "It is time we returned home. Now."

Isabel stared at her father, eyes wide. He almost never spoke to her with such command, especially not since she had begun assuming duties as mistress of the house. Even prior, he and Mama both had always been of the opinion that a gentle word did far more in service of disciplining a child or admonishing a friend to truly remedy unsuitable behavior.

As it turned out, her energy had been spent. Isabel did not resist as Papa took her arm and navigated her through the enormous building with great urgency, leaving poor Aunt Matilda huffing behind them to keep up until they emerged onto the front steps.

"I suppose this is where I shall leave you," the dowager countess said, cooling herself with a fan from her reticule, looking pointedly from the man to the girl and back again. "But, if you would prefer I come with you…"

Papa shook his head, his full cheeks quivering.

"That is kind of you, sister, but we should not impose upon your day any longer than we already have, what with you accompanying Isabel to a luncheon and then to Somerset House. I can manage from here, as is the plan."

"What can you mean? It is never an imposition, you know that," Aunt Matilda replied, eyes narrowing. They darted to her niece, silently inquiring.

Isabel did not raise her head. In fact, she did not know how long it had hung limply between her shoulders, bobbing about as Papa dragged her up and down more halls and stairs than she cared to count even.

"We have some matters to discuss at home," said Papa with that same sternness as before, his gaze resolute.

The lady stared at her relatives for a long moment before slowly nodding. "Very well, then. Should either of you change your minds, you know how to reach me."

She gave Papa a smile that did not hide her unease, squeezed Isabel's lifeless hand, and turned in the other direction to her approaching carriage. Taking charge of Isabel once more, perhaps sensing her disoriented state, Papa guided her toward their own coach, which had already been brought round, and helped her in.

Neither of them spoke as the carriage carried them to the main street. They both stared out their respective windows, father brooding with furrowed brows and daughter reeling from the numbness that she knew would break the moment she reached her quarters.

Eventually, a thought occurred to Isabel, so inconsequential compared to all the others racing through her mind and piercing her heart. She latched on to it, perhaps desperate for a moment of normalcy, and finally looked at her father.

"What became of Mr. Hawkins, Papa? I thought we were to bring your friend from Somerset House to dine with us tonight."

In truth, Isabel knew she should have been a little ashamed that she had not thought to ask after the kindly gentleman sooner, especially when she imagined him wandering around that huge place in a confused search for his companion.

Papa turned away from the window, his expression softening into the benevolence that was far more familiar to Isabel as he gave her a soft smile.

"You have always been such a sweet, thoughtful thing," he said quietly. Were his eyes…misting? "You inherited all the best parts of your mama, dear Isabel. Her boundless heart and her insatiable curiosity. I am always glad to see both so alive and well in you."

"Papa…"

"Do not worry about Hawkins. I explained, and he was extremely understanding. He shall send for his own carriage to convey him home and dine with us another night."

"Explained what?"

Even as she asked, Isabel dreaded the answer. What could have put her lovely, jolly Papa in such a strange mood? Her fingers, curled tightly around each other in her lap, ached from the anxious twisting she tried to hide.

The shadow of a passing row of tall townhouses threw the older man's gaze into darkness once more. He glanced away from Isabel.

"I, too, overheard what Lord Wrighthall and those others had to say about the earl's intentions."

Papa paused and swallowed, as if carefully deliberating his next step. Isabel's eyes widened, her trepidation increasing.

"I am afraid," he continued with a heavy sigh, "that I have been hearing increasing whispers amongst Society's gentlemen, but no one ever seemed certain of anything. So, despite my existing misgivings, I was hesitant to cast judgment upon the fellow—at least on that score. We are all well acquainted with these whimsical notions that sweep through the *ton*, more often than not with no basis in reality or practicality."

"And now?" Isabel somehow forced the question out in a painful, shallow breath.

"Now, well…"

Papa's eyes met Isabel's once more. She wished they hadn't. All she could see in them was the unbearable truth that would shatter the heart and hope that she had so carefully rebuilt.

"It is obvious that Lord Murfield is leaving again. I am so sorry, my darling daughter."

Isabel exhaled sharply, unable to close her shocked mouth, as if someone had landed a blow to her stomach. She had known what her father would say, yet it still hurt so much worse than she could have imagined.

"How can this be?" she mumbled to no one in particular, knowing there would be no satisfactory answer.

How could Caleb kiss her and tell her he'd never stopped loving her mere days ago all while still planning to quit Society again at the end of the Season for who knew how long— seemingly with the entire world but Isabel?

Could there be any chance that someone or something had been mixed up along the way to create such an impression?

"I wish I could make sense of it myself, but we both heard Lord Wrighthall. He is the earl's oldest and closest companion. He was the only one to know where Lord Murfield had gone and why."

Squeezing her eyes shut, Isabel held up a hand and nodded quickly. It was as if Papa had read her thoughts, though she did not need the remainder explained. Of course, if anyone was privy to the latest developments of Caleb's maneuvers—whether relating to travel or matrimony—it would be his best friend. He had certainly made no mention of it to Isabel despite claiming to renew their friendship.

Papa fell silent and reached out, taking Isabel's upraised hand

and cradling it in his, always warm and always comforting. She shuddered, the cracks in her heart deepening and widening, on the verge of breaking apart entirely.

For the remainder of the ride back to their townhouse, Isabel's mind imprisoned her in an endless loop between searching for some minuscule chance that the situation was not as it seemed and wondering how it could possibly be anything else. She could hardly breathe for the tears choking her.

This felt all too familiar. In an instant, those old memories that Isabel had been making a concerted effort to leave behind had come hurtling forward with full force. Only this time, they came paired with newer memories from this Season, forcing Isabel to inspect every recent interaction for signs of impending tragedy she had happily ignored, just like last time.

As Isabel's sense of having fallen into the trap of repeating history solidified, Papa held her hand in commiserating silence. He did not loosen his grip as he helped her down from the coach, waving away the footman who approached to do the job. Nor did he loosen it as he guided her up the front steps and into the foyer.

The front door closed behind them, shutting out the noise of the city. Isabel paused and looked up at her father with beseeching eyes.

"What am I to do, Papa?"

For a flash of a moment, his face crumpled in paternal pain before smoothing again into sympathy and reassurance. Papa grasped Isabel's upper arms and turned her to face him.

"Perhaps it is best if we took our leave of London…and its influences…early this year. The peace and quiet of the country may be just the thing for you now. Take some time to rest and think of what it is you truly want."

Isabel threw a glance over her shoulder at the closed door. Could it be that simple, that easy, to walk away without a word and never see Caleb again?

It had seemed that way for him four years ago…but now Isabel knew the truth of the immense pain that had driven him to do so.

Would she be making the exact same mistake for the very same reason? It did not feel necessarily like a mistake at present, not with the agony seizing her chest.

"But...perhaps I should at least speak to him first..."

Isabel could not stop those pitiful words from slipping out in one last feeble attempt to fight for the dream she'd only just begun to believe in again.

"My poor, poor girl." Papa sighed as he pulled his daughter into a crushing embrace.

Instinctively, Isabel's arms came up to wrap around him, her head burrowing into the comfortable crook of his neck.

"I do not know that that is wise. I saw how terribly he hurt you before, and how unwanted his reappearance was to you. And now this. How can I allow him the opportunity to bring you pain after knowing what he is capable of? Even we fathers have things we cannot bear."

Only then did Isabel's tears begin to flow. She squeezed her father tighter. "Thank you, Papa. I do think I wish to return home."

Home. To Bainbridge.

It would always be a permanent fixture in her life. Unlike Caleb. She flinched against the stabbing pain of that reality.

Papa untangled himself from Isabel's grasp and cupped her cheeks, round like his own.

"Why don't I help you up to your room? You rest, and I shall ready the household for our departure by midday tomorrow."

Isabel only had enough life left in her body to nod. Without another word, Papa wrapped an arm around her shoulders and steered her up two flights of stairs to the family wing. Outside her bedroom, he took her face in his hands once more and planted a soft kiss atop her head.

"Rest, my dear. I love you and will always protect you," he whispered into her hair.

She knew before the door clicked shut behind her that she

would not rest. It would have been impossible, even if the leather portfolio of Caleb's maps and artwork spread open across her writing desk had not been the first thing her eyes had landed on. A watercolor of an old palace sat at the top.

Just last night, cozy in bed with the deepest and most wonderful sense of completeness, Isabel's fingers had traced over its rough and earnest brushstrokes. She'd fallen asleep imagining herself there with him, experiencing corners of the country she had only read about in books or letters. When she had awoken, she'd found everything carefully transferred to her desk, most likely by her lady's maid.

Feeling as if her bones had been turned to brick, Isabel dragged herself across the room. Tears blurred her vision and streamed down her face as she collected the folder and its contents and unceremoniously dropped them onto her bed to be dealt with later.

Isabel slumped down into the chair without a care for proper posture, buried her face in her handkerchief for a moment, and pulled out a neat stack of blank sheets. She would not be the one to disappear without a word…but even she did not possess the courage to deliver those words herself.

CHAPTER TWELVE

ANOTHER BUMP LANDED against Caleb's knee, more insistent this time. He swatted at Wrighthall's fist and missed entirely. Confusion and melancholy had dulled his sense of accuracy.

"Will you not leave me be?" he grumbled as he adjusted himself in his chair like a sullen child.

"You are the one who told your butler to show me in when I called," Wrighthall rebutted, shifting closer to the edge of his own seat and leaning forward, propping his elbows atop his knees. "I believe I am owed an explanation for running all about London after you yesterday and never being allowed to catch up. Might it have anything to do with this despondent air about you?"

Caleb gritted his teeth and rubbed his forehead. Dear Wrighthall was too much in the habit of being right.

"I offer my sincerest apologies, my friend, I do. But it is too shameful for words. *I* am too shameful."

Silence filled the drawing room, still appointed in his brother's tastes.

"I am surprised at you, Murfield."

Frowning, Caleb glanced at the other man. He was surprised by the humorlessness in Wrighthall's voice.

"I thought—I certainly hoped—that you had learned by now," the baron continued.

"What is it that I am meant to have learned?"

Wrighthall sat up straight and eased back into his chair, arms crossed. "How soon you forget what happened the last time you withheld information from those who seek to help," he said with a weighty sigh.

A prickle of defensiveness inspired Caleb to straighten in his seat as well. He fixed his friend with a warning glare.

"That was an entirely different situation. Of that, you are well aware."

"Different in subject matter, I expect. But I am also entirely aware of the negative ramifications you endured as a result. I should hate to see you—or that young lady—suffer needlessly again."

Caleb shot to his feet. "It was not needless—"

"You know it was not right of your brother to swear you to maintain his secret. Nor was it right of him to delay telling you the truth and failing to adequately prepare you for your future while he was still able."

Wrighthall rose more slowly and fixed Caleb with a regretful expression.

"You lost years of happiness with Miss Abbott because of it. Had he been clearer-headed when you came to him, I do not believe the late earl would have wished for that outcome. If we cannot be free to share the entirety of our existences, pain and shame and all, with those we love, are we truly free?"

Silence stretched between them once more. The tension in Caleb's muscles eased ever so slightly. "I should discover which philosophers you have been studying of late," he mumbled under his breath.

"My favorite philosopher to study is always this one here," said Wrighthall, tapping his temple. "I shall ring for tea—no, something stronger, I should think—and you shall tell me what happened yesterday."

A few minutes later, Caleb did just that, both men settled into their chairs by the window once more. As he spoke, the intervals between Wrighthall's sips of port grew longer until he eventually abandoned his glass entirely.

"I told you it was shameful."

Wrighthall shook his head. "I wish I could say that Mr. Abbott is only seeing what any concerned parent might, but..."

Cold dread gripped Caleb. "You mean to say that you believe he is correct? That I am destined to repeat my mistakes and bring misery to Isabel?"

Wrighthall shook his head again, this time looking strangely abashed. "Not at all. In fact, I have never been more certain that Mr. Abbott is incorrect. But I must confess I am beginning to fear now that this interest in your movements has reached his ears and made him fearful of a repetition of the past.

"And I may or may not have been accidentally contributing to the impression of your impending departure, only because I have not heard you mention a change in plans. I said as much yesterday in the sculpture room to a few gentlemen who knew of my connection to you."

Caleb reached for Wrighthall's glass on the side table between them and thrust it at his friend. "That is no fault of yours. You provided what information you had. I should have canceled long ago, but my happiness was so great that I had entirely forgotten what it felt like to wish to leave."

"Will you call on Mr. Abbott and explain?" Wrighthall asked after downing a relieved gulp.

"Will my explanation of the present misunderstandings absolve the crimes of the past?"

"I will remind you again that you have committed no crimes, Murfield."

Caleb could not help scoffing at his friend's limitless capacity for humoring him. "What greater crime can there be than breaking the heart of the woman you love? What sentence can any judge pass that would remedy it?"

"If you explained the circumstances to the man—the *true* circumstances—perhaps he would find it in himself to be understanding. He has lost someone he loved, has he not?"

In Caleb's misery and self-pity, it was a tempting suggestion, though not tempting enough.

"But…But what if he is correct? What if I have already proven that I do not deserve her? What if I ruined my chance to make her happy four years ago and have only been deluding myself—both of us—since my return? When she looks at me with such sweetness and trust, how can I live peacefully knowing the pain buried beneath them?"

With a deep inhale, Wrighthall set his drink down once more. He leaned across the space between them and tapped Caleb's knee with his fist yet again.

"Because, while Mr. Abbott may have been watching you for signs of a potential threat, I was watching Miss Abbott." He paused and gave a strange, rueful chuckle.

"Lately of the two of you, it seems you are the only one who thinks yourself unworthy. She looks at you with sweetness and trust because you *already* bring her joy by sharing your life with her. She forgave you. Does that not mean you are permitted to forgive yourself? I fear that if you do not, then you truly will be sacrificing both your opportunities at happiness."

For the first time since that moment at the Royal Academy yesterday, Caleb's mind quieted. That was sorely tempting, indeed.

To forgive himself for his mistakes seemed far too easy. Otherwise, Caleb would spend the rest of his days, whether they were spent beside Isabel or not, feeling that he could always be doing more to make amends.

"A note has just been delivered for his lordship, with a request for urgent response," announced a voice at the drawing room door.

Caleb waved the footman in and took the single folded sheet from the silver tray. When he turned it over, he was surprised to feel a pinch of disappointment that a swan in purple wax did not greet him. At present, he certainly would not have minded if an older, wiser guide would simply reveal to him the right course of action and the right way to feel, anonymous or not.

Still, both he and Wrighthall raised their brows at the unfamiliar burgundy seal. Caleb popped it open with a letter opener and read the few lines in a blink.

"Well, who is it and what is their urgent business?" prodded the other gentleman.

"It is Lady Ainsworth. She has requested that I meet her at her residence at once. No reason given."

Wrighthall's brow rose higher still. "Very odd. Well, I suppose you had best ring for your carriage."

Before Caleb could gather his senses enough to find his footing, his friend had already crossed to the nearest bell pull and tugged. Caleb still had not fully regained his composure by the time Wrighthall pushed him into his barouche, or even by the time the horses slowed to a stop outside the dowager countess's townhouse.

He sat inside the relative privacy of the carriage for a moment longer, staring up at the handsome building through the window and willing his innards to cease their spinning. Though they had often encountered each other at various events throughout the Season, both with and without Isabel's presence, Lady Ainsworth had never personally written to Caleb, let alone summoned him to her home.

Would Isabel be inside, waiting for him? Perhaps she would be waiting to inform him that she'd thought better of the risk of entrusting her heart into the very hands that had shattered it into pieces.

"My lord?" asked his attendant from outside, voice muffled through the thick wood of the barouche.

"Yes, yes, I am ready," Caleb lied, more to himself than to the footman who opened the carriage door.

Lady Ainsworth's butler wasted no time greeting his lady's visitor and showing him upstairs, much to Caleb's regret. He still had not decided what he would say when he entered the drawing room...and found a most unexpected sight.

"Lord Murfield, thank you for joining us with such haste," said the dowager countess from the middle of the room, flanked by three young ladies.

"Good afternoon," Caleb replied, bowing his head to Lady Ainsworth, Miss Reeve, Miss Gardiner, and Miss Clara in turn.

Only when he'd taken his seat in the chair opposite the ladies' sofa did Caleb notice that unassuming Miss Gardiner clutched his portfolio in her lap. His heart plummeted, taking with it whatever weak hopes Wrighthall's encouragement had attempted to instill.

"What has happened to Isabe—Miss Abbott?" he asked quietly.

"She has left London, I am afraid," said Lady Ainsworth.

That unexpected answer stole the breath from Caleb's lungs, as if she had taken all the air in the city with her. Isabel was gone? Why should that surprise him? He would have run, too. He had been running away from himself for years.

"Did she say why?" he asked dumbly. He already knew what the answer would be. He was the cause.

"In truth, I believe her father may have had some influence there, given some recently acquired information," Lady Ainsworth replied. The corners of her mouth twitched down in a frown that seemed disapproving—though of her brother-in-law or the young man sitting across from her, Caleb could not tell.

"Sh-She also wished for these to be returned to you…should they be useful to you on your next journey," stammered Miss Gardiner as she presented Caleb's portfolio to him, eyes on the low table between them.

His suspicions had been confirmed. Hands numb, Caleb accepted the portfolio and mumbled his thanks to the girl. He ran his palm over the smooth leather. When had Isabel's hands last touched it?

"I do not blame her, or Mr. Abbott, but I wish I might have spared her a little pain with an explanation…"

"See! I knew there must be some sort of reason!" cried the younger Gardiner sister, hopeful eyes shining.

Caleb held up a hand and gave a humorless chuckle. "I would not be inclined to think too well of me just yet, Miss Clara, but I thank you regardless.

"You see, I had initially planned to end my Season early under the assumption that it would all end up as an exercise in misery after Miss Abbott gave me the cut direct the moment she saw my face again. But when that did not happen, to my utter disbelief..."

"Because you still love each other after all this time," Miss Clara added with a romantic sigh, hands pressed to her heart. She muffled a surprised yelp when Miss Reeve, seated to her right, jabbed her in the side with an elbow.

Caleb mustered a reassuring smile for the young lady. It had no effect upon his own wounded heart, which crumbled a little faster with every imagined gallop of the horses that carried Isabel away from any further hurt he might cause.

"That has been my most earnest, most ardent hope," he confessed slowly, lowering his head. "Still, I am afraid the shadows of the past continue to cast doubt upon the present and the future. I cannot say there is no logic in that."

"But is there?"

The unexpected sharpness in Miss Reeve's voice caused Caleb's head to snap back up. The other three ladies also stared at their companion in surprise.

She ignored them, her observant, brown eyes fixed squarely on Caleb. He went still. The viscount's daughter had spoken but three words to Caleb and he already felt quite put in his place.

"I pray you will forgive my bluntness, my lord, but the time for pleasantries has come and gone," she continued with an admirable, quietly confident fire.

"Mercy," Miss Clara, glancing nervously at Caleb, hissed in a whisper. Her wonderfully agreeable nature seemed to desire harmony at all times, even when harmony would have been wholly unnatural in the situation.

The older woman in the room, and the one most likely to be most concerned with proper decorum in the presence of a gentleman, merely watched with cool interest. Lady Ainsworth seemed to sense that Isabel's friends could manage the topic with both the honesty and delicacy required of it and made no motion to intervene.

"Please do not think to spare me," said Caleb, gesturing for Miss Reeve to continue.

"Then please do not think to plunge our dear Isabel into a lifetime of shrouded sorrow. Eventually, she attempted to convince us all that she'd healed, but we are her closest friends. Of course we could see the fractures that remained. It is high time they were healed once and for all…and you are the one to do it."

As Miss Reeve spoke, Caleb's lips slowly parted in shock. She had declared her intentions and he had requested not to be spared, yet he still had not expected such directness from Isabel's friend. Lady Ainsworth watched Miss Reeve from the corner of her eye, wearing a small, proud smile. The two other misses nodded along eagerly.

"What a fool I have been," Caleb said under his breath. "What a mess I have caused. What if that is merely who I am—a fool who is bound to bring her despair?"

"She is already despairing as we speak," answered Miss Gardiner. The room went still and quiet.

"She is?" Caleb repeated.

A cruel hand gripped his chest and twisted at the thought of his poor Isabel, suffering by his hand yet again. Perhaps, even now, she was drowning in tearful agony.

"Of course she is," Miss Gardiner replied, her tremulous voice barely more than a whisper. If she noticed the surprised glances her companions shared, she did not allow them to impede her rare surge of bravery.

"Do you not see, my lord?" the young lady continued with a kindness and patience that somehow reassured Caleb where no other well-meaning words had. The knot of unshed tears burning in his throat loosened ever so slightly.

"Isabel despairs because *you* are the very cause of her joy and she fears she has lost you...again. Indeed, she was angry and deeply hurt when she summoned us to say our farewells this morning. She thought you had willfully omitted your plans for the end of the Season, thus confirming a pattern of behavior that both she and Mr. Abbott much feared."

"Which we, of course, knew could not possibly be right," offered Miss Clara earnestly. "We have seen the way you look at her and the way you speak to and about her. Nothing can be clearer than the fact that you love her as unwaveringly as she loves you."

Miss Gardiner smiled softly.

"My sister is correct. Regardless of the unfortunate events that occurred in the past, none of us have any doubt now that you will devote yourself endlessly to the pursuit of Isabel's comfort and contentment for all her days, as she deserves. In a way, you are already doing just that."

"How so?" asked Caleb, his natural curiosity tempering his incredulity. He leaned forward in his chair.

Something deep inside him tingled, waking up, as if it sensed the imminent discovery of the true key he'd been searching for.

Seemingly startled by his sudden intensity, the young lady shrank into herself and swallowed but did not lose courage.

"You seem to think that by ceaselessly punishing yourself, you are somehow increasing Isabel's chances at happiness by freeing her from the constant reminder of your past mistakes and saving her from any potential mistakes you might commit in the future.

"At least in my view, which may not account for much, your own happiness is what will secure Isabel's—not your punishment. She is the most joyful any of us have ever seen when you are near. Yet if you continue to think that you will be doing the honorable thing by disappearing from her life again, I fear our dear friend's days of joy will be well and truly over. Even now, I do not believe Isabel would wish for you to withhold peace from yourself for all eternity."

Time seemed to slow around Caleb as Miss Gardiner's sage, compassionate words echoed in his ears and seeped into the cracks of his heart. They joined with Wrighthall's earlier sentiments, expanding to fill those old, hollow places.

He desperately longed for those sentiments to be true, that it might be possible—permissible, even—for him to release the burdens that had kept him and Isabel asunder for so long and find joy on the other side, in the smiles he hoped to put on Isabel's pretty lips every day.

"Do you mean to tell me that I should..."

Before Caleb could gather his thoughts enough to finish the question, a footman marched into the drawing room and announced to his mistress that her most important trunks had been loaded onto the carriage and the remainder would be following as swiftly as the staff could finish packing.

Lady Ainsworth thanked and dismissed him and rose quickly, the younger women following suit. Caleb did the same. The dowager countess, normally calm and composed, took a bold step forward, stopping just a few feet before her guest.

"Yes, Lord Murfield, that is precisely what we are telling you. The fight need not end here, but that is something only you can determine." The lady paused and placed a gentle hand on his forearm. "I hope to see you again soon. Very soon."

As the young ladies also excused themselves, a strange, welcome weightlessness filled Caleb's limbs. It did not completely drive out his fears, but it loosed their iron grip just enough for an ember of hope to shine through.

That little flicker, all the braver for its trembling, grew with every step that carried him out of Lady Ainsworth's drawing room.

Perhaps this was Caleb's chance to choose his fate. Perhaps he was finally finished with being swept about by waves of cowardice and grief and dragging innocent hearts underneath the waters with him.

He could choose differently. For Isabel's sake, he would.

CHAPTER THIRTEEN

THE FRESH AIR of Bainbridge, perfumed with the scent of early summer blooms, should have been a balm to Isabel's soul. As she trudged up the front steps of Woodruff Hall, Isabel knew it would not be so easy. Papa had advised her to reflect on her own wants and needs, but all she wanted and needed was Caleb.

She could not begin to fathom what would happen next or how she would heal from it. She had not fully healed from the last time, though she had tried to pretend otherwise.

Would Caleb always leave her behind in his plans?

"Dearest, would you like me to have a tray sent to your room?" Papa called after her.

Isabel glanced over her shoulder to find even absentminded Lewis and little Maria watching her with pity. All she could manage in response was a limp wave of dejection, which she repeated inside the house to every servant who inquired after her needs and health, some with genuine concern.

By the time she'd reached the family wing and her stinging eyes landed upon the door to her quarters, Isabel ached in every muscle from the effort of maintaining an upright posture. The many hours of travel over bumpy roads surrounded by her family and sleeping in unfamiliar inns had not helped. Finally, she arrived in the welcome solitude of her bedroom. She could attempt to make sense of this all in private.

Only she was not alone, not exactly. On the middle of her

four-poster bed sat a letter.

Mind, spirit, and body exhausted, Isabel dragged herself the last few steps across the large room and slumped against one of the posts, loosely wrapping one arm around it. Heart hammering with its last vestiges of energy, breaths coming in shallow and ragged, Isabel perched on the edge of her bed. Slender fingers slipped across the smooth cream blanket and gripped the folded sheet by the corner.

A purple swan, just as she had expected. Of course, she'd also recognized the handwriting after scrutinizing her first letter for so long that the entirety of the English language had ceased to have any meaning. Something about that swan in the wax always made the mystery feel more tangible.

Isabel swallowed against the tears building in the corners of her eyes and in her throat and opened Lady Swan's second letter. The more she read, the blurrier her vision became as the tears sprang forth. Though she could only bear to read it once, a particular line lodged itself into Isabel's mind immediately.

"Just when the challenges seem insurmountable, the clouds may break in the most spectacular and unexpected way. Begin looking to the future instead of clinging to the past. History will only repeat itself if you allow it."

Tossing the letter to the other side of the bed, Isabel allowed herself to tip over and land amongst the blankets with a muffled *thump*. She turned onto her side and burrowed her hot, sticky face in the soft fabric.

"History will only repeat itself if you allow it."

Those words swam before Isabel's tear-filled eyes as she lay curled up on her side, deserted and miserable, in a bed that suddenly felt too large.

Yes, Isabel had allowed history to repeat itself. It had been a dreadful mistake. She had all the proof of that fact right here in the burning pain and confusion that lanced through her, scorching hot and frigid cold by turns. It was all too familiar yet somehow even more potent than before.

Lady Swan may have known much, but clearly, the information regarding the Earl of Murfield's travel plans had escaped her notice. If the matchmaker knew that Caleb had already arranged to leave, surely, she would not be so irresponsible as to delude Isabel into thinking that any hope remained.

Unless, of course, Lady Swan had come into some other, more recent intelligence…

After some unknown time, Isabel managed to push herself back up into a seated position, not quite upright just yet. She glanced to the window. The light streaming in was golden, heavier. At least a few hours of wallowing and wondering must have passed.

With another great effort, she forced her legs to support her, then carry her across the room to her writing desk in the alcove. It had not been so terribly long ago that she had done this very same thing in her room in London after receiving Lady Swan's first letter.

How much had happened since then! How much her feelings, once thought to be immovable, had transformed in such a short time! In the end, Isabel may yet discover that none of it had been worth it. She pulled out just two sheets from the drawer and dipped her pen in its inkwell.

If she had learned her lesson last time and remained committed to her material goals, she would not have found herself in this position. She would not have been forced to wonder where she stood with the man who would be her husband. A tear fell to the page before she could stop it.

Despite all the time and effort she put forth into expanding her mind and knowledge, Isabel had still allowed herself to be fooled. Not once, but twice.

And here came Lady Swan—not once, but twice—attempting to fill Isabel's head and heart with nonsense that should have been done away with years ago as a youthful fancy.

Another tear dropped to the paper with a whisper-soft landing. This time, she could not bring herself to care. It did not matter. These letters would be short, just a few lines. She could write around the wet spots.

Her dearest friends, the ones who had known her all her life and knew the intimate details of her particular situation, would no doubt be obliged to side with Isabel now, no matter how tempting it had been to abandon logic in favor of whimsy and romance. She only wished Mercy, Ellen, and Clara could join them in Bainbridge as well and complete their circle once more.

To Isabel's relief, her sweet lady's maid did not linger or raise too much alarm at her mistress's state when she answered the bell and collected the letters. These past few days, Byrd had been especially tender in Isabel's care without suffocating her in it.

Alone once more, Isabel forced herself to pace while she awaited responses. While the movement was helpful for her body after days in a carriage, it did little to improve her spirits. Just as Isabel had begun to wonder if she would in fact be hearing from either Lydia or Felicity today, Byrd's familiar knock sounded at her door.

"They have finally written back?" Isabel demanded as she swung it open herself.

The older woman took a startled step back and shook her head. "No, miss. They are here. Well, they are in the foyer. Swinton sent me to inform you when they spied Mrs. Harrowsmith and Mrs. Wheadon coming up the drive."

For the first time in what already felt like years, Isabel's heart pulsed with a flicker of true relief. "Thank you, Byrd. Please show them up."

"To the drawing room, miss? Would you like tea sent in as well?"

"To my quarters. But yes, a tray of tea and sandwiches, if you would."

Surprise flashed through Byrd's eyes before she nodded, curtsied, and hurried down the hall. Isabel waited in the doorway. When her friends appeared at the top of the stairs, a small smile worked its way onto her lips. She rushed toward them, her eagerness to crush them in an embrace increasing with every step.

Until something in Lydia's arms caught her eye. Isabel slowed, unable to remove her gaze from the bundle of blankets. Just for a moment, all her own concerns disappeared, almost as if the clamoring of her muddled thoughts might somehow disturb that peaceful slumber.

"Is this…?"

Lydia beamed a grin that Isabel had never before seen on her friend's naturally stoic features, her blue eyes brimming with joy.

"This is our little Miss Mary Harrowsmith. Would you like to hold her?"

"Very much so, but first let me look at you," Isabel replied, turning to her other friend.

Felicity, too, glowed with an inner happiness that was like nothing Isabel had ever experienced. Even the golden curls framing her face, now fuller than her twin's and beautifully soft, seemed to shimmer. She rested a hand on her protruding stomach, draped in silk folds of rich red.

"I must look a little different since you last saw me." Felicity chuckled before grimacing and rubbing at the lower curve of her belly. "Apparently, this one wishes to make its presence known to you—and to dance a quadrille upon my insides."

The other woman took Isabel's hand and placed it in the same spot. Half a breath later, she felt the swift bump of a tiny foot or fist, surprisingly forceful. Her smile widened.

"I would expect nothing less of *your* child. But I pray for your sake that the next one tends more toward your husband's temperament. Come, both of you."

A moment later, the three friends settled into chairs in Isabel's room with a platter of refreshments. Their newest addition stretched and yawned in the protective cradle of Isabel's arms. Her eyes widened in wonder as she cooed incoherent syllables at the darling girl and brushed her impossibly soft, dark hair with the tips of her fingers.

"Being a mother looks well on you, Lydia," whispered Isabel over Mary's perfect, drowsy face. "And it shall look just as well on you in a few months, Felicity. My heartiest congratulations to you both!"

The eldest of their group, the first of them to embark upon all these strange, terrifying, incredible journeys, watched her daughter from her seat under the window with pure pride. Felicity wore a similar expression as she smiled down at her round middle, absentmindedly stirring her tea.

"Thank you, dear Isabel," replied Lydia without removing her eyes from Mary. "But I must ask, why has your family returned from London almost a month sooner than we were expecting you?"

"Careful, Lydia," said Felicity with her characteristic teasing smirk, "or Isabel may be in danger of feeling that you are not utterly thrilled to have her home, as I am, naturally."

Lydia pursed her lips at Felicity. "Of course I am just as thrilled to have Isabel here. You were the one who would not stop suggesting increasingly unlikely and bizarre explanations during our walk here."

"Such as?" Isabel demanded. A giggle attempted to start in her throat. She had missed these two and their often contradictory dispositions dearly.

"Oh, something or other to do with a duel. At least Mary was sound asleep in her pram at the time. She is far too young to be hearing of duels," Lydia grumbled, though she could not hide the glint of humor in her eyes.

Felicity laughed aloud, uninhibited. She waved a dismissive hand through the air. "Atticus has recently introduced me to a new author of adventure novels. Each one contains at least one dramatic duel, which help quite effectively to distract me from the less pleasant aspects of this condition."

"I also required distraction from my back pains and swelling feet around your time. I must admit I am happy to be done with those days for a while," Lydia added with a shudder.

"But Lydia is correct," Felicity continued. "We were both quite shocked to receive your summons and curious to discover its meaning."

Isabel deflated. It had been too easy to lose herself in her friends' lives and cease thinking about her sorrows for a moment. Lydia set down her teacup and reached for Mary, palms up. Isabel carefully transferred the baby back to her mother's arms.

Adjusting Mary's blankets around her tiny form, Lydia resumed her seat. "Lord Murfield?"

"And our old friend, Lady Swan." Isabel reached to the writing desk beside her and picked up the letter. "I know both of you will be inclined to agree with her, but I fear that she is unaware of the most recent developments."

The married ladies exchanged a concerned glance, their expressions growing more severe as Isabel explained the Season's events from the beginning, including much that she had been unable to fit into her frequent letters to Bainbridge. They shook their heads in disbelief as Isabel's chronological retelling reached the morning of the Abbotts' sudden flight from London.

"This is odd, indeed," mumbled Lydia, instinctively swaying back and forth to maintain Mary's restful state.

"Based on your recent letters, I would never have guessed Lord Murfield to be capable of this, not a second time," Felicity added with a scowl that seemed equal parts confused and angry.

Muscles suddenly heavy, Isabel allowed her head to hang. "If he could manage it once, then he shall always be capable of managing it again...clearly. Papa certainly thinks so."

"Dear Isabel," Lydia said with a sympathetic sigh. "I am so sorry you have been burdened with this, and that we could not have been nearer to assist you through it."

Isabel quickly shook her head and swatted at the tear that had sprung to the corner of her eye.

"Neither of you is to apologize for that. But do not attempt to agree with Lady Swan's recent encouragements simply because you are converts to her abilities."

"I suppose you cannot blame us," Felicity replied with a light chuckle, patting her stomach. "And this from a woman who, just a year ago, abhorred the very notion of romance! I should like to think, especially after my own experience, that Lady Swan takes extreme care with her encouragements and would not steer you toward the possibility of despair."

Lydia gave a subtle nod of agreement, careful not to jostle Mary. "Both Felicity and I reached similar points, remember? Lady Swan is wise in ways we cannot see—and may never discover. Nor does life reveal the nature of its unfolding until the precise right moment. Your moment may yet come."

Isabel looked down at her lap and twisted her napkin in her hands.

"Perhaps she simply made an error with me. Perhaps Papa is correct. The past contained every clue I needed to predict this outcome, yet I was too foolish to see the truth.

"Besides, what will he think when he learns I am gone? He may be relieved that he's been spared from facing me himself. Or angry that I have done the very same thing to him that caused so much bitterness in my own heart."

"In either case, he would not be deserving of you," stated Felicity firmly before softening. "Of course we only want your happiness, Isabel, and will continue including it in our daily prayers...when I do not doze off before I finish mine. You know you shall always have our support."

Such sweet words coming from Felicity in particular began to stir Isabel.

Lydia nodded her agreement. "Whatever happens, you are stronger than you know and will find a way to make a happy life. Time will prove it."

Bittersweet gratitude formed a lump in Isabel's chest. They were right. Isabel prayed she would come to feel that with greater certainty in the coming days. Even if she never found happiness with Caleb, she would always have her precious friends and family. She would cling to that pinprick of light with everything she had. It had been the only thing to keep her afloat before.

A thud and voices raised in alarm downstairs caused the three ladies to jump. Mary released a heart-wrenching wail. Her mother immediately sprang to her feet, bending at the knees in a gentle bounce as the baby wriggled to free herself of her suddenly unwelcome blankets.

"Wait here," Isabel commanded before quitting the room. She had not made it halfway down the hall before a maid scurried up the stairs at the other end. "Louisa, what was the cause of that commotion just now?"

The girl, likely a few years younger than Isabel, struggled to hide her smile. "A few rather unexpected guests have just arrived downstairs. Of course, I cannot be sure I heard rightly about the one, but my eyes are convinced..."

Isabel's brows furrowed. "Who has arrived?"

"Lady Ainsworth, your friends Miss Reeve and the Misses Gardiner, and two gentlemen. They say one is an *earl*, miss."

A rush of air swept past her as Maria raced toward the stairs, her governess following at as brisk a pace as she dared.

"Come back here at once, child!" snipped the woman.

"*Please*, Miss Oakley, I wish to see *some* of the guests," Maria whined over her shoulder. "Tell her, Isabel! Tell her that French can wait until the guests have gone!"

Isabel did no such thing. Her mind was too blank to do anything but force her to follow.

CHAPTER FOURTEEN

CALEB'S CHEST STILL heaved from the effort of leaping down from his carriage, running up the front steps of Isabel's country home, and keeping his legs steady before the father of the woman he loved.

"Thank you for admitting me," he said in as measured a tone as he could manage despite the deafening buzz of his heart.

Mr. Abbott watched Caleb with narrowed eyes.

"It is the least I could do, seeing as you came all this way," he said, though he did not yet extend the invitation of a seat in his study. "May I inquire as to why you have followed my family all the way to Kent?"

Nerves trampled Caleb's stomach. He forced a deep inhale. The time had finally come to face the impossible and do the right thing when every voice of reason inside him screamed for him to turn and run. This time, Caleb would not obey, even when he knew his defeat was all but written.

"I owe both you and Miss Abbott an explanation and an apology."

After another excruciatingly long moment of examination, the older gentleman held out a hand toward the chair across from his desk. "You will explain to me first before I allow you to see my daughter, you understand."

"Yes, most certainly. I did wish to do just that, for I know I can have no hope with her without your acceptance," Caleb answered in a rush as he perched on the edge of his seat.

Mr. Abbott leaned forward and planted his elbows heavily on his desk. "Forgive me, my lord, but do you mean to say that you still intend to pursue Isabel? Do you truly think that wise?"

Caleb swallowed against the jagged rock in his throat and prayed with everything in his heart that whatever spilled forth from his mouth would at least be coherent.

"I do not know what is wise any longer, but I know what is true," he began with a shaky breath. "It is true that I have made many terrible mistakes, and my guilt will always exist in some part of me, even if I were to be blessed with this forgiveness—which I know is not owed to me in any way."

He paused for breath. Did Caleb imagine that the cold suspicion and quiet anger in Mr. Abbott's eyes had softened?

"It is also true that, from this day forth, Miss Abbott will never doubt my desire—my *need*—to be by her side and use all my resources of wealth and mind to foster the happiness she has always deserved."

"Then why did you abandon her the first time?"

That familiar sensation of danger flooded Caleb every time he considered revealing the truth of Daniel's death. He offered another prayer, this time to beg his brother's forgiveness, and confessed.

"And so I kept secret the reality of my brother's decline, even from the kindest, most understanding soul in the world," he finished, ignoring the crack in his voice.

Mr. Abbott's full brows inched up and he rubbed his ruddy cheek. "Goodness, that is a very sad tale, indeed. I am sorry to hear it. Losing a loved one so young… It is no easy thing to bear. You have my sympathy, my lord."

"Thank you," Caleb whispered.

"Still, why did you stay away for so long?" the other man asked, his frustration tempered.

Caleb pressed his lips together and lowered his head.

"That is the more challenging question. I suppose I was in

mourning and not of sound mind. Time passed and my shame grew while I attempted to dull my grief with constant exposure to new places and sights. None of this excuses my behavior, of course."

Silence filled Mr. Abbott's drawing room for several moments, or perhaps it was a mere blink. Caleb had lost all sense of time. He could only focus on taking the man's questions and concerns as they came and answering with honesty and humility.

Eventually, Isabel's father nodded and looked down at his desk. His unreadable gaze lingered on a delicate silver filigree frame, angled away from Caleb's view.

"Well, I cannot say I do not understand that. None of us is sound in grief. The desire to run… I felt it, too, when I lost my Rebecca on the very same night she brought us our darling Maria."

"I have heard nothing but loving praise for Mrs. Abbott. I am sure her loss shall always be felt keenly, and I am sorry for it," Caleb offered quietly, imagining the portrait of Isabel's beloved mother on the other side of the frame that had caught Mr. Abbott's attention.

Icy dread shot down his spine as he reeled his mind away from that dark corner. If his sanity had nearly been destroyed from the loss of his brother, he did not dare think he had any hope of surviving a loss such as Mr. Abbott had suffered.

The older gentleman's eyes darted up to his visitor's face, their familiar kindness slowly returning. He moved the frame.

Normally, Caleb might have blushed to realize he'd been caught staring. Instead, he found himself staring with even more unabashed intensity.

The late Mrs. Abbott had been exceedingly handsome, with a serenity and sagacity in her gaze that was all too familiar to Caleb. To her eldest child, she had also given the starkly contrasting beauty of her coloring, from the porcelain complexion to the deep-black hair to the bright-green eyes that could cut through any room and silence any fear. From Mr. Abbott, Isabel had inherited her round, soft features.

Together, they had made a stunning woman with the most enchanting, gentle, brilliant spirit—sheer perfection such that the world had never seen before or would again.

Until perfection repeated her wonderful qualities in a child of theirs, of course after Caleb and Isabel had taken their time to enjoy each other's company after their lost years. Was it still too soon for Caleb to turn his thoughts toward the possibility of that future?

"I only wish all the children looked precisely like her, though Isabel comes nearest," said Mr. Abbott, startling Caleb out of his reverie. "They have no need of my features when I may see myself in a mirror any time I wish. But to see her in them…"

He paused and looked at the young man across from him once more, returning the frame to its usual spot. "Knowing that my wife lives on in Isabel's sharp mind and Lewis's love of entertaining distractions and Maria's confidence is, perhaps, what made the crucial difference for me."

"How so?" Caleb asked.

Mr. Abbott's attention drifted back to his wife's portrait. "It was not easy, by any means, as I am sure you can imagine. I will also admit my own guilt in leaving the children for as long as I did to the care of their aunt, Rebecca's dear sister, who was in mourning herself. So you see, I understand what it is to lose oneself after such a tragedy and cause greater struggles for those around us.

"But I daresay they helped me return to myself sooner than I may have otherwise done. I love them dearly and did not wish to see them lose both their parents. Rebecca would have haunted me had I allowed such a thing to happen."

Mr. Abbott chuckled and paused again. Caleb could not decide if his smile was fond or bittersweet. Most likely both. The other man returned his gaze to Caleb.

"Now that I truly consider it, I realize I have thought more harshly of you than you perhaps deserve."

Hope stirred. Caleb's heart jolted.

"We were all deeply saddened to hear of your brother's passing when the news reached us. And now I have a better understanding of why you disappeared. You did him proud by protecting his secret as best you could, which you can trust will remain safe with me as well. But seeing how upset my Isabel was, I failed to give thought to the fact that you—barely more than a child yourself—had just buried your last close relation."

Caleb's heart jolted again. To his surprise, there was no pain at the mention of Daniel. Only his awakening hope remained.

"It was a lonely time of life. With Daniel's permission, my good friend, Lord Wrighthall, did much to see me through those early days and weeks and ensured that I did not wholly abandon my new responsibility. After that, he visited me from time to time and kept me abreast of the most important happenings in Society…and some of Miss Abbott's happenings. I only wished to know that she was well.

"Still, I had never felt quite so alone. Not only am I an orphan, with both parents gone before I had memory of them, but I am no longer a brother."

"Heavens, the weight of grief and a title on unsuspecting shoulders! I am quite glad that is a situation I need never contend with," Mr. Abbott exclaimed quietly as he leaned back in his chair and crossed his arms loosely over his chest.

"It was much like the rest of it," Caleb admitted with a glum smile. "Time passes and you realize you have somehow continued living, after all."

Silence stretched between the two men once more. A pensive expression overtook Mr. Abbott's features as he nodded slowly. Caleb waited.

"There is one last thing I do not understand. Are you not scheduled to quit London and take a merry band of fellows with you about the country?"

"Yes, and no." Caleb shook his head with a wry chuckle.

By the time he'd finished explaining, Mr. Abbott's eyes had

gone almost as wide as the face of the clock on the mantel behind him. He, too, shook his head and barked out a laugh.

"Leave it to the *ton* to concoct their own wild story and convince each other to run away with it! I thought that could be the case, but I was so worried for Isabel. Would you forgive me, my lord, for assuming the worst and acting in haste?"

Caleb couldn't help the grin spreading across his face and waved a hand in dismissal.

"You acted out of love and responsibility to your child, Mr. Abbott. And, as you rightly said, you had every reason to think Miss Abbott in danger of being harmed again. I seek no apologies and shall accept none, for I am the sole guilty party."

The lightness spreading through Caleb's limbs almost had him convinced that he'd succeeded. Isabel herself could still reject him, for which he would never blame her. Yet Caleb immensely appreciated her father's willingness to listen and understand, no matter the day's outcome.

All too soon, Caleb's panic returned. Mr. Abbott grew serious and propped his elbows atop his oak desk once more. He did not look at the younger man, his gaze fixed on something beyond, thoughtful.

"Do you promise that you will never make my precious daughter despair again? Do you promise that you truly will do everything in your power to secure her daily happiness?"

Every muscle in Caleb's body sprang into action. He hovered over the very edge of his chair, hands gripping the carved armrests.

"I do promise, to the best of my ability, whatever the requirements. She shall never again shed a tear of sorrow on my behalf. If I could contrive it, she should never have occasion to shed any tears but those of the purest happiness. Alas, I know well enough that I cannot ask for so much in the course of life, but I will ask it regardless with every prayer, for her sake."

Mr. Abbott's small smile disappeared behind his steepled fingers. "A rousing argument, indeed. Have you any closing statements for me to ponder? Or questions, I should say?"

That was the final jolt Caleb's heart required. It began an unbridled gallop toward his most dearly held dream.

Without thinking, he rose from his chair. Mr. Abbott did the same.

Daniel had told him long ago that this was the sort of thing a man did standing on his own two feet, though he'd never had the opportunity to do so himself. Caleb prayed that his brother watched from above with pride and approval. For the first time since that awful day, Caleb felt this particular prayer had been answered.

"Mr. Abbott, may I request your daughter's hand in marriage…if she will have me?"

For some increasingly disconcerting reason, Mr. Abbott still did not look at Caleb.

"Yes, you may request her hand. As for the other part, well, perhaps that is best left to her, do not you think?"

There was no time for relief to wash over him.

"Caleb…"

The glorious racing of his heart stilled to a peaceful, natural rhythm. He turned to the door.

Isabel was here and all was right in the world.

CHAPTER FIFTEEN

CALEB GASPED. "WHY are you here?"

Isabel almost laughed. The scene that met her eyes was too bizarre, the surrounding situation too large in her mind, to permit such levity just yet. She could hardly believe what she was seeing or what she had just overheard.

"I believe I am the one who should be posing that question," she replied in quiet awe.

Caleb gulped, his Adam's apple bobbing and cheeks reddening. He blinked his beautiful, sweet eyes at her.

"Yes, of course. This is your home and your father's study. Of course you should be here. Forgive me, please."

The sensation his familiar voice inspired in her hollow chest forced Isabel to turn her face away quickly. Its depth and warmth spread through that hollow space like a well-worn blanket being unfurled and laid down with care.

Just hours ago, Isabel had begun the work of resigning herself to the possibility that she may never again hear it, or see that inquisitive, sincere gaze or those enchantingly vivid, red waves.

Yet here Caleb Smythe stood, baring his soul to her father and asking for her hand. It was all too much. It was all too...wonderful.

Isabel inhaled sharply and squeezed her eyes shut. When would she awaken from this unfairly convincing dream?

She felt his presence instinctively before she opened her eyes.

No other sense but that of her heart would ever be necessary to know the man she loved—had always loved and could never stop loving—was near.

"Isabel…"

Cautious hands hovered just over her bare arms. Isabel could no longer resist. She allowed herself to look at him.

What she saw in his stare made her heart soar. She could feel her lips parting in astonishment and desire and was powerless to stop them.

It had never been more clear. Caleb loved her. He was devoted to her. Isabel could feel that truth in her bones.

Yes, he had loved her in the past, yet the missing years had given a profound depth to the appreciation in his expression. It assured her that she could entrust him with her heart once more…forever.

A gruff cough from the other end of the room distracted the young pair only just enough. Neither of them jumped or removed their focus from the other. They merely turned their heads slightly in acknowledgement.

Mr. Abbott chuckled. "I am touched to have been involved in this sweet moment, but please continue it in the drawing room with your aunt and friends, I beg you."

"May we walk about the grounds instead?" Caleb asked.

"Keep within view of the house," answered Papa.

There, in the most unexpected place, her father's study in sleepy little Bainbridge, Caleb grinned and offered his arm to Isabel as if it were the most natural thing in the world.

Isabel grinned back and accepted. It *was* the most natural thing in the world.

They walked leisurely through Woodruff Hall, assured of finally having all the time together that they desired.

"Here they come!"

"Are they smiling?"

"But I cannot see—"

"Careful, you stepped on my foot!"

"Please do not cry, sweet Mary!"

Eager voices and a shrill whine spilled from the drawing room as the couple approached. They beamed at each other and laughed quietly to themselves. Without exchanging a word, Caleb and Isabel agreed that they wished to revel in their delightfully obvious secret for a while longer.

"It was so thoughtful of you to bring my friends to me. Poor Lord Wrighthall might be experiencing a bit of a shock." Isabel giggled, imagining the amusing scene unfolding behind the wall.

Caleb chuckled. "I thought you might need them today, either way. But it is all thanks to your aunt for convincing their mothers to allow it, particularly Lady Eldmar. Do not worry on Wrighthall's account, however. He will manage well enough. You should see the packs of ladies Wrighthall's mama throws at him."

When they swept past the open door of the drawing room, five heads peeked out and watched them go with what Isabel assumed was nearly unbearable curiosity. A sixth countenance hovered in the doorframe just behind them, ever watchful and ever hopeful.

The feeling of being by Caleb's side once more, of knowing that her place would always be by his side, was so sublime that Isabel nearly floated down the grand split staircase that led to the foyer.

"This way, to the back. We shall have better access to the grounds from there," she said when they'd reached the bottom step.

She also silently hoped that, since the windows in her father's study and the drawing room faced different directions, no one would come searching back here for a better view of their wanderings.

The gentleman stopped, forcing Isabel to stop alongside him. She looked up, her curiosity growing when she saw the shine in his eyes.

"First, there is something I wish to show you just outside the front doors."

Isabel arched a brow and followed her dear Caleb silently into the golden late afternoon sunlight and down the front steps. He untangled his arm from hers when they reached his carriage and opened the door.

"Caleb!" She gasped, covering her mouth with a hand, only allowing the barest hint of a tease into her voice.

"Is something wrong?" he asked, spinning around on his heels, a rectangular package clutched to his body. Despite being almost half Isabel's height, the thing didn't seem terribly heavy in Caleb's strong grip.

She pressed her other hand over her heart, reveling in this playful familiarity she'd once thought they would never share again.

"My lord, you cannot simply whisk me away just yet. We are not married. In fact, we are not *truly* engaged. But I suppose you have intentions to rectify that?"

The handsomest, most animated grin spread across Caleb's face. "I have every intention to rectify that and much else, miss."

Without thinking, Isabel's hand shot out and grasped his forearm. She felt his surprised inhale as his gaze darted down to the spot where she touched him.

"I do not wish for you to spend the remainder of your days kneeling before me, you know. Have we not revisited the past enough? Can we not look forward to the future now? *Our future?*"

As the words spilled from Isabel, her grip tightened. Perhaps she would simply never let go. It felt too good to have no distance and no barrier between them, not even a glove.

With a soft smile, Caleb angled his face lower until their foreheads almost touched. His eyes held her as a willing captive, enveloping Isabel in a depth of love that mirrored her own.

"I know, sweet Isabel. It is yet another reason you are an angel descended from heaven. But nothing would bring me greater joy than to bring you joy in any way I can. On that note, may I?"

He adjusted the unwieldy package in his arms and Isabel quickly led them around the spacious house to the nearby garden fountain. Warmth radiated through her body when they sat upon one of the firm, stone benches that surrounded the fountain, their backs to the house.

The vibrancy of the world around her fell into perfect harmony with the sheer elation within. Caleb's hand slowly reached across Isabel's lap and took hers, threading their fingers together. The feeling of their palms pressed tightly, their thighs and shoulders brushing, took her breath away.

They sat like that for some time, savoring each moment, until eventually Caleb remembered his mysterious gift propped against the end of the bench. He said nothing as he untied the twine and removed the plain, brown paper at what Isabel considered to be a cruelly relaxed pace.

When he caught her angling her head this way and that for a better look, he narrowed his eyes at her over the gift in a playful warning that required no words. Isabel giggled, without tempering her volume or covering her expression.

She was at home, with the man she loved and to whom she would soon be betrothed—if he ever finished unwrapping that thing. Why should she hide this bliss away?

Finally, Caleb dropped the remainder of the brown paper, only to reveal the back of a canvas.

"This here is the only portrait I attempted to paint during my travels—and by far my best work. I met a newly married couple in Scotland, and upon observing me at work in a public square for some time, the husband commissioned me to try a portrait of his wife."

He turned the canvas to face Isabel. Eyes wide and mouth ajar, she took in the beautiful portrait. Each lovingly made detail was a testament to the skill of the artist…and his fascination with the subject.

"In the end, the couple chose not to take it. It did not bear a strong enough resemblance to the lady, you see."

Unable to remove her gaze from her own visage, Isabel laughed and shook her head. "Did she bear any resemblance to me?"

Caleb smiled sheepishly and rubbed the back of his neck. "Her hair was black, I remember. And her eyes were…blue? Hazel, perhaps. I am sure she was longer of face as well."

"In short, she may have barely resembled me from a distance," Isabel summarized, another wonderfully light laugh bubbling up and spilling out.

She took the portrait from Caleb and propped it up on her lap. From this close, she could see each brushstroke and where the oils effortlessly blended together. Layer upon layer, built over time, after much careful study and reflection. It had been a labor of love, indeed.

"I know you heard the majority of what I shared with your father, but I hope you will allow me to echo myself in some fashion, as I believe some points bear repeating."

Isabel set the portrait back in its wrappings and returned her full attention to the man seated beside her. Her heart swelled and hummed with anticipation as Caleb pressed himself even closer and took both her hands in his.

"I hope this may be proof to you—as it should have been to me—that no matter how far I went, there was no corner of the world where I could live in peace while knowing you still existed somewhere out there without me. I saw you in everyone and everything because I wished so desperately that you were there experiencing it all with me."

"Dearest Caleb," Isabel whispered.

She did not know when his face had come close enough that she could feel the heat of her own breath reflected off his skin. One of Caleb's hands came up to cup her face.

"I have finished with running. I attempted that method and somehow still ended up here before you in the end."

He paused and let his forehead rest against hers again.

"We were always meant to be here. Together. The vastness of miles and time could not prevent us from finding our way back to each other. I shall always, always cherish your forgiveness in the deepest part of my heart and look ahead with wonder to all that awaits us. Still, I shall always regret being the cause of such sadness."

"I am not sad now," Isabel said under her breath. "I can hardly remember that sensation. The contentment you have brought me these past several weeks—excepting the mishaps of the most recent few days—has completely erased all ills of the past. I promise."

"You are an angel, indeed. You shone your light through my darkest times even when I hid myself as far away as possible."

Soft, sweet, welcome lips pressed just above the space between Isabel's brows, often furrowed in thought yet perfectly relaxed now. They remained for a long moment. Isabel breathed into the kiss, into this sliver of time that belonged only to them. When Caleb pulled away, he looked into Isabel's eyes with an endearingly hopeful resolve.

"If it would be agreeable to you, I hope to share not only my griefs and continued education in the art of healing with you, but my joys as well—which I believe will quickly become innumerable if I am able to secure my chief joy. For none others may exist without it…without you. You are essential to my being."

Every inch of Isabel's body sang. Her spirit soared into the bright-blue sky above.

"It is not simply *agreeable* to me. Nothing could be more perfect. Nothing could better satisfy my greatest dream and most ardent desire since the moment we met at Hyde Park."

Isabel felt Caleb's smile. He pulled her closer.

"I love you so very much, Isabel. Always."

"I love you, too, Caleb. Forever."

"Will you do me the honor of spending the rest of time with me as my wife?"

Tears flooded Isabel's eyes. The moment she had been waiting for these four long years had finally arrived. Everything had fallen into place.

"Of course I will."

With the hand still cradling her face and the other around her waist, Caleb tilted Isabel's chin up and crushed her to his chest in one fluid movement.

His mouth found hers, a heavenly match. Isabel's arms slipped around his neck, her fingers into his hair.

Their kiss was slow, deliberate, exquisite. They had no need to rush. It was only their third kiss, yet Isabel marveled at how perfect and natural it already felt. And one day, hopefully soon, she would lose count of them entirely.

Soon the need for air compelled them to break apart, though their arms remained secured around each other in a comfortable hold. Isabel and Caleb smiled at each other, both aglow in resplendent sunlight and unshakable certainty.

They had done it. Despite every indication otherwise, they had weathered the storm and discovered a beautiful future awaiting them as the clouds broke.

"I suppose there are a number of people back in the house on the verge of going mad from anticipation," Isabel said after another moment of silent enjoyment.

Caleb chuckled and glanced at the looming shape of Woodruff Hall behind them. "I thought I saw some curtains fluttering suspiciously just now."

Arm in arm, Isabel's head occasionally coming to rest on Caleb's shoulder, the newly engaged couple returned to the house at a pace that proved too leisurely for their anxious companions. The eyes of their best friends and beloved family, including Lewis and Maria, flew to Isabel and Caleb.

"Finally, there you are! Will someone please inform us of what is happening?" demanded Felicity the moment they'd stepped foot in the drawing room. She even managed to shoot to her feet in indignation, wobbling for only the briefest second before finding her balance, a hand on her stomach.

"Sister, please be seated and allow them an opportunity to speak." Mercy groaned from the chair beside her twin.

Before Felicity could decide if she would obey or argue, a hushed gasp rippled through the room. Isabel's and Caleb's hands had become intertwined, their expressions no doubt revealing much.

"Thank you all for your patience, and for all you have done in aid of our happiness," Isabel began. Everything inside her tingled with excitement.

"'*Our* happiness?'" Clara repeated with a squeak.

Isabel offered her elated smile to each of her loved ones in turn, brimming with so many delightful feelings, it proved impossible to distinguish one from the next. Wrighthall, flanked by Isabel's curious siblings, watched in content stillness. The young ladies clung to each other. Papa and Aunt Matilda did the same. Isabel could not tell which of them was more eager.

"Yes, Caleb and I are engaged!"

Happy tears blinded her as their audience engulfed the pair in resounding congratulations. The world spun too quickly for Isabel to catch her breath. Or perhaps she had Maria, grasping her by both hands and twirling her in circles, to thank for this splendid dizziness. In any case, Isabel did not mind in the least.

Nor did she mind as their brother interrupted to gently pinch her cheek. "Well done, you. It's about time you remembered that you have a heart and not only a brain," he said with a teasing chuckle as he stepped aside for Papa.

"Congratulations to Lord Murfield and the future Lady Murfield!" cheered Papa as his strong arms squeezed a giggle from his daughter. The others applauded their hearty agreement.

"I am so thrilled for you, darling. As is your mama, I am sure," he added in a whisper meant only for Isabel. He tightened his grip around her once more and released her into the care of her five dearest companions.

They swallowed her in a sweet embrace, their arms entangled around each other with Isabel securely in the middle. She received the outpouring of their lifelong love and support with still more tears.

"Thank you, my girls," she whispered, her voice catching in her throat. "Now that I think of it, I do not know how I will manage without you all so near. If only you and your families could come with us to Berkshire."

Lydia, to her right, rested her temple against Isabel's. On her left, Mercy did the same. Clara burrowed her sniffles in Ellen's neck as the others pulled in even closer, as close as they could manage around Felicity's growing figure.

"No matter how far apart our paths take us, we shall always be part of each other's lives," said Lydia quietly.

"And now we are more tied together than ever thanks to a certain writer," added Felicity.

Clara lifted her head. "That makes the three of you. Some of us are still waiting on our letters."

An idea struck Isabel. She pulled away just enough to take a proper look at each of her friends' beautiful faces. They stared back, curious.

"The rest of you will receive them, I am sure of it. But are we not already our own little club? Like a...society. A society of swans."

Delight dawned upon five pairs of eyes.

Before any of them could speak, a familiar hand landed upon Isabel's shoulder. The girls released her. She turned to that gentle touch.

"What a truly wonderful day," said Aunt Matilda with a proud smile as she returned baby Mary to her mama.

"Thank you, my marvelous aunt, for the role you played in this day, which I intend to hear more about later."

Aunt Matilda waved a hand. "You give me too much credit, my lovely niece. I am of the firm belief that I merely expedited matters—and not by much, surely."

The dowager countess paused and looked to the sofa in the middle of the room where Caleb had settled beside Lydia, introducing himself to little Mary. If such a thing were possible, Isabel felt the size of her heart increase tenfold.

"He would not have given you up this time. I always knew he would come for you."

Isabel eased her hand into Aunt Matilda's. "I am glad you held to your faith when mine had all but disappeared."

Happy lines appeared at the corners of Aunt Matilda's eyes as she chuckled softly and leaned in with a whisper. At that moment, Caleb looked up, perhaps sensing Isabel's gaze. He excused himself from his conversation with Lydia and Mary, offered his seat to Ellen, who eagerly accepted, and crossed the drawing room. Aunt Matilda excused herself as well.

Isabel's future husband took her hands and brought them to his chest, holding them against his heart. "What wisdom did your aunt impart on you just now?"

As it did so often when Caleb was near, the rest of the world fell away. She cared not for who might see as she tucked her head under his chin and melted against him.

"There will be times in life when we need those closest to us to keep the faith we cannot. So long as we remember that, we shall never be lost."

Caleb hummed thoughtfully. "I wish I could marry you today with those very words."

"As do I. But it shall be worth the wait, I promise." Isabel laughed and burrowed a little deeper, allowing herself to become a little heavier.

Perhaps, in some small corner of her heart, Isabel had always known that truth. She was right where she had always belonged—in Caleb's arms, sharing a life and all the discoveries to come.

Yes, it had been worth the wait.

EPILOGUE

Isabel pressed her face against the carriage window as Osborne Park's towering, expansive beauty came into view. She marveled at the history it carried, to which she and Caleb would contribute and one day become part of.

"I hope you are pleased with your home, beautiful wife."

The horses slowed as they neared the end of the drive, gravel crunching under hooves and wheels. Isabel sat back against the plush seat and slipped both her arms around her Caleb, pulling him even closer.

"Of course I am pleased, charming husband, because you will be there. It is *our* home."

Caleb released a sigh of utter contentment as he rested his cheek atop Isabel's head. "Thank you for finally returning some life to this place. It was in dire need. As was I. Thank you for returning life to me, Isabel."

"Neither of you shall be without it ever again. I will see to that."

"Of that, I have no doubt whatsoever," Caleb replied with a chuckle that vibrated through Isabel's body.

The carriage stopped before the grand front staircase. A neatly groomed footman stood tall on one end of each step. One of them opened the door for his master and new mistress.

"Welcome home, my lord, my lady."

Similar polite greetings and congratulations followed them up the stairs. Each one sent a thrill through Isabel from head to foot. Though they had spent their first month of marriage wandering about the country, it still felt so strange to think of herself as Isabel Smythe, Countess of Murfield.

At least Aunt Matilda had reassured Isabel on her wedding day that eventually, she would find herself responding to the call of Lady Murfield without a second thought. It would become as much a part of her as Caleb himself was.

After an hour or two spent on a leisurely tour of the generous main floors, her husband paused before a final pair of mahogany double doors and smiled down at her. "Shall we?"

Isabel grinned and nodded without any idea what awaited on the other side. "We shall."

The doors swung inward to reveal Caleb's handsomely appointed office, with a massive desk lit by an arched window and enough shelves to qualify as a library. Somehow, though Isabel could not tell how precisely, it reflected him perfectly.

Caleb stepped in behind her and gently gripped her upper arms, his thumbs rubbing circles into her skin. He turned her around. There in the center of the wall, in perfect view of Caleb's desk, hung a silver filigree frame, identical in design to the one that housed Mama's portrait in Papa's study.

It was Isabel's portrait, painted by the loving, familiar hand of her husband, that looked out across the entrance and doorway of her new home, proud in a place of high honor. Isabel's happiness, both in the painting and in reality, blazed bright for all to see.

"What do you think?" Caleb asked.

"Well, no one can doubt that being in love has made me quite radiant."

Caleb spun her back around so fast that Isabel stumbled into his arms, laughing like a giddy girl experiencing the first bloom of love. Her husband brushed the curls away from her eyes and held her face in both his hands.

"Impossible. You have always been radiant. That is a mere mortal's attempt to emulate it in an infallible medium. But still, I will always be glad to hear that you are in love with me."

Shrugging a shoulder, Isabel laughed. "Be mindful of your wishes. You may tire of hearing how much I am in love with you."

Tenderly, Caleb's hand slipped down the side of her face, thumb and forefinger holding her chin in a loose grip. "You shall tire of hearing how much *I* am in love with *you* long before I do."

"I suppose even such well-matched minds as ours cannot agree on every subject," Isabel replied in a whisper.

"It is not necessary, so long as our hearts agree."

He kissed her, passionate and sweet all at once. They had only been husband and wife for a little over a month and Isabel had already lost count of their kisses.

When they pulled apart, husband and wife kept their arms looped around each other. Isabel smiled softly as she studied the details of Caleb's face and wondered how they would change throughout the lifetime ahead.

"Will my brilliant wife tell me what she is thinking?"

Isabel tilted her head to one side and continued observing.

"Paintings are wonderful and I admire the dedication required to create them, but at times like this, I wish we could capture a moment in perfect recreation with the blink of an eye, and perhaps even hang those recreations up on the walls."

Caleb gave that thoughtful pout that Isabel so adored.

"A fascinating and tempting idea, indeed. Though I am afraid if such a thing were possible, I would have no choice but to build an entirely new house for the sole purpose of functioning as a gallery. I would use every blink to capture your beauty."

Emotion flooded Isabel's chest, her eyes widening. "Then I should have to build one right beside yours."

"My lady?"

The newly married couple turned at the polite intrusion. The butler stood in the doorway, a small platter in hand. Isabel went still.

"I am sorry to disturb you so soon after your arrival, but this was just discovered outside. If you prefer, I will have it delivered in the morning with your breakfast tray."

Caleb's elbow prodded Isabel in the side. She stepped forward, accepted the letter, and dismissed the butler with thanks.

Lady Swan truly never failed. Isabel knew that to be true before she'd flipped the envelope.

"It's her," Caleb whispered in awe. Still transfixed by the amethyst seal, he led Isabel to two comfortable leather chairs in the corner.

A warm wave of contentment settled over Isabel as she opened the seal and read aloud to her husband.

"'Dearest Lady Murfield, I know I will not be the first to welcome you to your new home, but I hope I may claim the privilege of being the first to welcome you to this sacred moment of the blessed calm after the turmoil—not only of wedding preparations, but of the separate journeys you both undertook to arrive here.

"'There is never a better time than a marriage—the joining of two pasts into one future—to begin painting this fresh, blank canvas that stretches before you both. There can be no doubt that you and your clever husband will create the masterpiece you both deserve. Thank you for giving love, and each other, a second chance.

"'Yours always, Lady Swan.'"

About the Author

Penny Fairbanks has been a voracious reader since she could hold a book and immediately fell in love with Jane Austen and her world. Now Penny has branched out into writing her own romantic tales.

Penny lives in the Midwest with her charming husband and their aptly named cat, Prince. When she's not writing or reading, she enjoys drinking a lot of coffee and rewatching The Office.

Come follow me on Facebook to stay up to date on my latest news and coming releases.

facebook.com/pennyfairbanksauthor